Haddix, Margaret Peterson.

Among the betrayed.

$16.99

DATE			

AR Pts. 5.0
BL 4.8

AMONG THE BETRAYED

Also by Margaret Peterson Haddix

The Missing series

Book 1: *Found*

Book 2: *Sent*

Book 3: *Sabotaged*

The Shadow Children series

Among the Hidden

Among the Impostors

Among the Barons

Among the Brave

Among the Enemy

Among the Free

The Girl with 500 Middle Names

Because of Anya

Say What?

Dexter the Tough

Running Out of Time

The House on the Gulf

Double Identity

Don't You Dare Read This, Mrs. Dunphrey

Leaving Fishers

Just Ella

Turnabout

Takeoffs and Landings

Escape from Memory

Uprising

Palace of Mirrors

AMONG THE BETRAYED

MARGARET PETERSON
HADDIX

Simon & Schuster Books for Young Readers
New York London Toronto Sydney

First Aladdin Paperbacks edition August 2003

Simon & Schuster Books for Young Readers
An imprint of Simon & Schuster
Children's Publishing Division
1230 Avenue of the Americas
New York, NY 10020

Also available in a Simon & Schuster Books for Young Readers hardcover edition.
Designed by Greg Stadnyk
The text of this book was set in Elysium.

Manufactured in the United States of America
40 39 38 37 36 35 34 33 32

The Library of Congress has cataloged the hardcover edition as follows:
Haddix, Margaret Peterson.
Among the betrayed / by Margaret Peterson Haddix.
p. cm.
Sequel to: Among the imposters.
Summary: Thirteen-year-old Nina is imprisoned by the Population Police, who give her the option of helping them identify illegal "third-born" children, or facing death.
ISBN 978-0-689-83905-4 (hc.)
[1. Betrayal—Fiction. 2. Conduct of life—Fiction. 3. Science fiction.] I. Title.

PZ7.H1164 Ak 2002
[Fic]—dc21
2001032214
ISBN 978-0-689-83909-2 (pbk.)
ISBN 978-1-442-44306-8 (eBook)
0813OFF

AMONG THE BETRAYED

CHAPTER ONE

You were supposed to wake up from nightmares.

That's what Nina kept telling herself as she cowered on the floor of her concrete cell. All her life she'd had horrible dreams about being captured by the Population Police. Sometimes they carried shovels and scooped her up like trash on the street. Sometimes they carried guns and prodded her in the back or pointed at her head.

But she always woke up before anyone pulled a trigger.

Once she'd even dreamed that the Population Policeman who came for her was wearing Aunty Zenka's ruffled lace nightie, complete with a nightcap. For months after that dream Nina refused to give Aunty Zenka a goodnight kiss, and nobody understood why. Nina wouldn't say, because then everyone would laugh, and it wasn't funny.

Nina knew she was right to be terrified of the Population Police. They were the bogeyman and the Big Bad Wolf and the Wicked Witch and the creep-show monster and every other villain she'd ever heard of, all rolled into one.

But like the bogeyman and the Big Bad Wolf and the Wicked Witch and the creep-show monster, the Population Police belonged in stories and nightmares, not real life.

Now Nina banged her head against the cement wall beside her.

"Wake up!" she ordered herself desperately. "Wake up!"

The banging made her head ache, and that didn't happen in dreams, did it? In dreams nothing hurt. They could flog you until your back bled, and you didn't feel a thing. They could tie your feet together so you couldn't run, and the ropes didn't burn at all.

Nina's wrists and ankles were rubbed raw from the handcuffs and ankle cuffs that chained her to the wall. The skin had been whipped from her back; even the slightest touch of her shirt against her spine sent pain shrieking through her body. One of her eyes seemed to be swollen shut from the beating.

Everything hurt.

But it had felt like a nightmare, being arrested, Nina told herself stubbornly.

She savored the dreamy quality of her memories, as if her arrest had been something good—not the worst moment of her life. She couldn't even remember the Population Policemen coming into the dining hall or calling her name. See? See? Didn't that prove it hadn't really happened? She had just been sitting there eating breakfast, rejoicing over the fact that she'd gotten three whole raisins in her oatmeal. And then suddenly the entire room was deathly quiet, and everyone was looking at Nina. She could feel all those eyes on her; she dropped her spoon. Oatmeal splashed on the girl beside Nina, but Lisle didn't complain, just kept staring like everyone else. And it was those stares, not the sound of her name, that had made Nina rise, and go forward, holding out her wrists to be handcuffed.

Which name did they call? Nina wondered. *Nina or . . . or—*

No, she wouldn't even think it. Sometimes in dreams the Population Police could read your mind.

Nina went back to remembering, remembering how the other girls sat like dolls on a shelf while Nina walked down the endless aisle between the tables. The familiar dining hall had somehow turned into a canyon of eyes. Nina did not turn to the right or to the left, but she could feel all those eyes following her, in silence. Those eyes were like dolls' eyes, as blank as marbles.

Why didn't anyone defend me? Nina wondered. *Why didn't anyone speak out, plead, beg, refuse to let me go?*

She knew. Even if it was just a nightmare—it was, wasn't it?—she knew that everyone would have been too terrified to make a peep. Nina knew she would have been too terrified to speak, too, if it had been someone else dazedly gliding toward the man with the medals on his chest. Someone else being arrested. (Why was it her? How had they found out? Why was she the only one they knew about? *Stop,* she chided herself. *Nightmares never make sense.*)

She remembered how hard it had been to keep her feet moving—up, down, right, left, closer, closer. . . . She couldn't protest or defend herself, either. Opening her mouth, even just enough to let out a whimper, would have released hysterics.

Please don't kill me! I'm only a kid. I didn't want to break any laws. It's not my fault. Oh, and please don't take Jason. . . .

Now, in her jail cell, Nina clenched her teeth, afraid that she might still let those words spill out. And she couldn't. Someone might be listening. Someone might hear his name. Whatever she did, she had to protect Jason. Jason and Gran and the aunties. And her parents, of course. But she could hold her tongue about all the others. It was Jason's name she wanted to wail, Jason she wanted to call out to.

Jason, do you know where I am? Did you worry when I didn't show up at our meeting place in the woods? You're so brave. Can you . . . can you rescue me?

She was being so silly. This was just a dream. In a few minutes the morning bells would chime, and she'd open her eyes in her swaying top bunk at Harlow School for Girls. Then she'd brush her teeth and wash her face and change her clothes and maybe, just maybe, get four raisins in her oatmeal at breakfast. . . .

She remembered her arrest again. She remembered

reaching the front of the dining hall, facing the policeman. At the last moment, right before the policeman snapped the metal cuffs on Nina's wrists, she had noticed another man standing behind him, watching Nina just as intently as all her classmates were. But all her classmates had gone glassy-eyed with fear, their gazes as vacant as dolls'. This man's dark eyes said everything.

He was furious. He hated her. He wanted her to die.

Nina gasped. She couldn't pretend anymore. She remembered too much. She couldn't have dreamed or imagined or made up that look. It was real. Everything that had happened to Nina was real. She had real handcuffs on her wrists, real scars on her back, real fear flooding her mind.

"They're going to kill me," Nina whispered, and it was almost a relief to finally, finally give up hope.

CHAPTER TWO

"Why?"

The word exploded in Nina's ears, and she jerked awake. Then she jerked back because a man's face was just inches from hers, yelling at her.

"Why did you betray your country?" the man demanded.

Nina blinked. She was doomed anyway—why not argue? "Betray my country?" she could sneer. "What kind of a country thinks it's a betrayal just to be born? Was I supposed to kill myself out of loyalty? Out of patriotism? How is it my fault that my parents had two babies before me?"

But anything she said would betray her mother and Gran and the aunties—everyone who'd kept her hidden, everyone who'd kept her alive.

She didn't speak.

The man sat back on his heels. It was dark in Nina's prison cell; she thought it was probably the middle of the night. The man's silhouette was just a dim shadow in front of her. *He's a shadow and so am I,* Nina thought. She was still groggy enough that that seemed funny.

Then the man turned his head and murmured, "Now." Instantly the entire cell was flooded with harsh, too bright light from the one bare electric bulb overhead. Nina squeezed her eyes shut.

"I know you're awake," the man said softly. "You can't hide."

Nina stiffened at that word, "hide." He knew. Of course he knew. Why else had she been arrested? She thought she'd resigned herself to dying, but suddenly she was drowning in panic. Was this it? Was the man about to shoot her? Or was he going to take her somewhere else to die? How did the Population Police kill illegal children?

Nina opened her eyes a crack because it was better to see her killer than to cower sightlessly, expecting a gunshot at any moment. But seeing gave her another jolt: She recognized the man. He was the one who'd been there when she was arrested, staring at her with those hate-filled eyes.

Weakly Nina closed her eyes again. It didn't matter. She still had the man's image imprinted in her mind. He was tall and muscular and richly dressed, like someone on TV. His dark hair waved back from a high forehead. He looked powerful, just as Jason always looked powerful. But Jason had never once looked at her with such hatred.

Nina remembered something Gran always said: "If looks could kill . . ." *Looks can kill, Gran,* Nina wanted to say. *That look's going to kill me.*

The man chuckled.

"I don't care if you talk or not," he said. "Your cohort already told us everything. *He* cracked like an egg. I just thought you'd like the chance to tell us *your* version. Maybe your friend lied a little to save his own skin. To make himself look a little better and you, well, a lot worse. Guiltier. You know?"

The man was practically crooning in Nina's ear; his face was so close to hers that she could feel his breath on her cheek. Nina could barely think. What was the man talking about?

For a minute Nina didn't even understand the words he'd used—"cohort"? What was that? Then she remembered all the mystery novels Aunty Lystra had read aloud back home, on nights when the TV wasn't working. The detectives in those books were always accusing people of being "cohorts in crime." Cohorts were partners, helpers. Did he mean Gran and the aunties, who were cohorts in hiding her?

Nina barely managed to keep herself from gasping. *No!* she wanted to scream. *You didn't catch them. You couldn't have!* Tears began streaming down her face, silently.

But the man hadn't said "cohorts" and "they" and "them." He'd said "cohort." "He." "Him."

Nina knew only one him.

No, she corrected herself desperately. *I met other boys from Hendricks School. Just because I didn't really know them, that doesn't mean they didn't betray me. In fact, it makes it more likely that they turned me in.*

Nina thought about the guys she and her friends had sneaked out to meet in the woods at night. As a group, they were as skittish and timid as rabbits. She couldn't imagine any of them having the nerve to speak to the Population Police.

Except one.

No! The denial slammed through her brain. Maybe she even screamed it aloud. Even if you forgot that Jason loved her, even if you forgot that he'd kissed her, secretly, by moonlight—he was an illegal third child, too. All of them were, all the kids who met in the woods. Even if they wanted to, it would be too risky for any of them to betray her.

Maybe it's my father, Nina thought bitterly. *Maybe Gran was wrong and he did know I was born, did know I exist. Maybe he thought he'd get a reward for turning me in.*

Nina opened her eyes, angry enough now to face the hating man without flinching.

The man was smiling.

"Oh, Scott—or should I say *Jason*—had some very interesting tales for us," the man said cheerfully. "He made you out to be quite the operator."

Nina screamed. The sound echoed in her tiny concrete cell, one long wordless howl of rage and pain.

When she stopped screaming, the man was gone.

CHAPTER THREE

If morning came, Nina had no way of knowing it. She sat for hours, stiff and sore and heartbroken, huddled under the harsh light of the one bare bulb.

People always say that death's the worst thing that can happen to you, she thought. *It's not.*

She wished the man had just killed her and been done with it. She could have died—well, not happily, but at least with something to clutch on to, something to believe in: *Jason loves me. Oh, Jason, my beloved, good-bye!* In the time since her arrest, she realized, she'd begun picturing herself and Jason as the kind of tragic, star-crossed lovers who inhabited Aunty Zenka's favorite books and TV shows.

Gran and the other aunties always made fun of Aunty Zenka for liking those books and shows.

"Oh, give me a break!" Nina could remember Aunty Lystra complaining one evening when Aunty Zenka was reading aloud by candlelight. "Why doesn't the beautiful, vivacious heroine just tell Jacques, 'Hey, you've got incurable TB. Life's too short to hang around watching you die. Ciao!' "

"Because they're in love!" Aunty Zenka had protested. "And love is—"

"A load of garbage," Aunty Lystra finished for her. Aunty Lystra worked for the sanitation department. She was always comparing things to garbage.

Nina had felt sorry for poor, sentimental Aunty Zenka, who could get misty-eyed in the first seconds of one of her shows, with the first sentence of one of her books. But now Nina thought Aunty Lystra must be right. Aunty Lystra would think Nina had been a fool to trust Jason in the first place.

But he was so nice to me, Nina defended herself. *And he was so strong and handsome, and he knew so much. . . .*

For the first time Nina thought to wonder: *How* had he known so much? He'd known that the woods were a safe place to meet. He'd known about Harlow School for Girls. He'd known the exact right time of day to slip a note under the front door of the school, when the girls were walking to class. So a girl, not a teacher, would find his note.

Nina had been that girl. She lost herself, remembering. Two months ago, in the hallway at Harlow School, she'd scooped up a folded-over page that other girls had walked right past. She'd held the cream-colored, heavy-weight paper in her hand for a long moment, daydreaming about what it might be. She'd known it was probably nothing interesting, nothing that concerned her: a notice about electric rates, maybe, or a government edict about the size of spoons in the school kitchen. But as long as she didn't open it, she could imagine it was something exciting—like Cinderella's invitation to the prince's ball, perhaps. And since *she* was the one who'd picked it up . . .

The suspense had been too much. Nina had slid her finger between the edges of paper, breaking the seal. Carefully she'd unfolded the page and read:

To all Harlow girls
who are concerned about shadows:
Please join the like-minded students of Hendricks School for Boys
for a meeting at 8 P.M., April 16,
halfway into the woods between our schools.

Nina had never heard of Hendricks School. She had never been in the woods—any woods. Except for the day she came to the school, she'd never been outdoors at all. She was a little worried about the word "shadows." Did it mean what she thought it meant? Was this dangerous?

But Nina didn't really care. She knew instantly that she was going to that meeting. She would have gone if the note had said, "To all Harlow girls who are concerned about hammers." Or "fruit flies." Or "pencils." Or "prehistoric civilizations' development of canals and aqueducts"—the subject she'd just ignored in her last class. Nina felt like she'd been waiting her entire thirteen years to receive this invitation.

Convincing her friends was a little harder.

"We're not supposed to go outside," Sally said timidly when Nina whispered her secret after lights-out that night.

"Nobody ever *said* that," Nina argued, trying to keep her own panic out of her voice. If her friends refused to go, would she have the nerve to go alone?

"They never said, 'Don't brush your teeth with toilet water,' either, but that doesn't mean I'm going to do it," Nina's other roommate, Bonner, argued.

Sally was tiny and golden haired, and Bonner was tall and dark and big boned, practically burly. Since Nina was medium height and medium weight, with medium brown hair, she always felt like the link between the other two. When they walked down the hall together, Nina was always in the middle. When the other two disagreed, Nina was always the one who suggested a compromise. Having both the other two oppose her made Nina feel a little desperate.

"Look, they want to talk about shadows," Nina said. Even in the dark she could tell that both of her friends froze at the sound of that one word. Harlow School was full of secrets that everyone knew but almost never discussed. At the beginning of the school year, when Nina was still horribly homesick, she'd amused herself by imagining Aunty Rhoda, her most practical aunt, materializing in the dining hall at breakfast or lunch or dinner, and marching up to the front of the room to lay out the truth for everybody:

"Fact: Every single one of you girls is a 'shadow child'—

a third or fourth or maybe even fifth child whose very birth was illegal because the Government doesn't allow people to have more than two kids.

"Fact: All of you came here with fake I.D.'s certifying that you are somebody else, somebody the Government thinks has a right to exist.

"Fact: Anyone with half a brain could see you're all pretending. Half the time the blond, Swedish-looking girl forgets to answer to the name, Uthant Mogadishu. And she's not the only one. All of you cower at any mention of the Government. All of you tremble any time the door opens.

"Conclusion: So why don't you all just drop the little charade and talk about it? Tell one another your real names. Talk about your real families, not the pretend brothers and sisters and parents you've probably never even met. Compare notes on how you managed to hide, all these years, before you got a fake I.D. Console one another about the difficulties of coming out of hiding, instead of lying in bed each night sobbing silently, pretending you don't hear your roommates crying, too."

But of course Aunty Rhoda was miles away, and Nina wasn't brave enough to stand up and make that speech herself. Still, with Sally and Bonner, in the dark of their room at night, she'd dropped hints, and they'd dropped hints, too. All school year it'd been like following the trail of bread crumbs in the fairy tale—Nina had never learned very much at any one time, but by spring she knew that

Sally had two older sisters and a house by the seashore and parents who were working with the Underground, attempting to overthrow the Government. And Bonner had a brother and a sister and a huge extended family of aunts and uncles who all lived in the same apartment building and took turns taking care of Bonner.

"They want to talk about shadows," Bonner repeated. "Right. So do the Population Police. What if it's a trap?"

"What if it isn't?" Nina hissed. "What if this is our only chance?" She prayed the other two wouldn't ask what it was a chance *for*—she'd never be able to explain. Maybe Sally and Bonner had never gotten to the point, in hiding, where they wanted to scream at the four walls around them. Maybe they hadn't read and reread and re-reread all the fairy tales where princesses were released from magic spells and evil enchantments. Maybe they'd never thought, even at Harlow, *Oh, please, there's got to be more. This can't be all my life is.*

"Look, you can take your I.D. card with you into the woods," Nina said. "The Population Police can't do anything to you if you have your I.D. card. And we don't even have to talk to these boys. We can just hide behind the trees and watch them. Just come with me. Please?"

"Oh, all right," Bonner said grimly.

"Sally?" Nina asked.

"Okay," Sally said in her smallest voice. Nina knew that if there'd been even a glimmer of light in the room, she would have been able to see absolute terror in Sally's eyes.

For once Nina was glad for darkness.

So they'd gone into the woods, clutching their fake I.D.'s like lifelines. But they hadn't just hidden and watched. They'd met Jason and his friends. And Jason had told them a wonderful story about a girl not any older than them, Jen Talbot, who'd led a rally demanding rights for third children like them. Jen had been brave enough to tell the Government that third children shouldn't have to hide. Jen had died for her beliefs, but still, listening to Jason's wonderfully deep voice praise Jen, Nina had wanted to be just like her.

But now that Nina had been arrested, it looked like Sally and Bonner had been right. The woods had been dangerous. The three of them shouldn't have stepped foot outside Harlow School. Nina should never have met Jason, never have kissed him, never have fallen in love.

"No!" Nina found herself screaming again. "No, no, no, no, no . . ."

CHAPTER FOUR

The hating man came back. Nina stared at him coldly, her eyes like slits, her chin held high.

"You're the one who lied," she said. "Why should I believe you? You can say anything you like. But I know. Jason wouldn't betray me."

The hating man wouldn't meet her gaze. He glanced to the other side of her jail cell.

"Why haven't you eaten?" he asked.

For the first time Nina noticed a tray of food just beyond her feet. Two thick crusts of black bread, a smear of synthetic butter on each, were stacked on a plate with a small, wormy-looking apple. It was no worse than the food she'd eaten at Harlow, or at home.

"I wasn't hungry," Nina said defiantly, and it was true. But now that she looked at the food, her stomach rumbled.

"Right," the man said with a disbelieving snort. "Hunger strikes aren't terribly effective when you're condemned to die anyway."

He spoke so casually that it was all Nina could do not to gasp. So it was true. They were going to kill her. Fine.

But they couldn't make her die hating Jason.

The man rocked back on his heels and squinted at Nina, like a naturalist studying an interesting bug. For a while the Government had been big on the idea that everyone should eat insects, so they'd shown a lot of bug shows on TV. Nina had never thought to feel sorry for the bugs being studied.

"So," the man said. "Is Nina Idi your real name?"

No! Nina wanted to scream. It would feel so good to tell the truth now, at the end. Nina had always loved her real name, Elodie. Elodie Luria. When she was really little, Aunty Zenka had even made up a song about Nina's name: "You're just like a melody . . . Our little Elodie." Elodie was a fairy-tale name, a princess's name. When Gran and the aunties had scrimped and saved and finally gotten enough money to buy Nina a fake I.D. on the black market, Gran had come home and laid out the I.D. card on the table like a golden prize. Nina had tiptoed over and read the name, with all the aunties and Gran circled around like the good fairy godmothers at Sleeping Beauty's christening. Then Nina had begun screaming.

"Nina Idi? That's my name now? That's like . . . like Ninny Idiot! You want me to be a Ninny Idiot?" Even screaming, Nina had felt ashamed. That little rectangle of plastic was her ticket to freedom. It represented twelve years of Aunty Lystra wearing glasses she couldn't see through anymore, twelve years of Aunty Rhoda wearing the same coat, twelve years of Gran darning socks so many times the socks were more darn than sock. Twelve years of all of them living on stale bread and thin broth. Still, Nina couldn't help feeling that the precious card was her death sentence instead of her reprieve. If she wasn't Elodie anymore, if she was supposed to be this strange new person, Nina Idi, then she wasn't Aunty Zenka's little melody, she wasn't Gran's little sweetiekins, she wasn't the one beloved ray of sunshine in an apartment full of tired old women. She wasn't anybody at all.

Somehow, amazingly, Gran and the aunties had recognized Nina's screaming as fear, not brattiness. They'd all crowded around her, hugging her, comforting her, "You'll always be our special girl, no matter what. Even when you're away at that school. . . ."

And just hearing that word, "school," Nina had understood that Nina Idi really was killing Elodie Luria. Elodie could exist only in Gran's apartment. Nina was the one who was going to leave.

But now if Nina Idi was about to die, wouldn't she rather die as Elodie?

It was so tempting.

"That's not a tough question," the man chided her. "Are you Nina Idi or not?"

"You're the one who arrested me," Nina snapped, just to buy some time. "Don't *you* know my name? Maybe you didn't even arrest the right person!"

The man turned around.

"Guard?" he called toward the door. "A chair?"

Minutes later a guard appeared with a solid wood chair that the man slid into. He leaned back in it, obviously enjoying the greater comfort. Nina still huddled on the cold concrete floor. The guard left, locking the door behind him.

"I decided this conversation might be worth continuing longer than I wanted to spend squatting on your putrid floor," the hating man said, as if it were Nina's fault her jail cell was dirty. He leaned toward her, resting his chin on his hands, his elbows on his knees. "Now. Surely you realize my question wasn't as stupid as you imply. After all, the other criminal we arrested yesterday morning, Scott Renault, was masquerading as Jason Barstow, pretending to be an illegal third child who'd gotten ahold of a fake I.D. *Supposedly* he was trying to trick other illegals with fake I.D.'s into revealing their true identity so he could report them to the Population Police. Got all that? His story, of course, is ludicrous. Everyone knows that in this great country of ours it's impossible for an illegal to get a fake I.D. No law-abiding citizen would defy our beloved Government so flagrantly."

Nina stared back at the man in confusion.

"What . . . what was I arrested for?" she asked quietly.

"Treason, of course," the man said, almost cheerfully. "You betrayed your country."

"How?" Nina asked again.

"Hey, who's supposed to be asking the questions here?" the man protested. He answered her anyway: "You and this Jason—Scott?—what should I call him?"

"Jason," Nina whispered. "He's Jason."

"Okay. Whatever. You and this Jason tried to trick the Population Police into paying you for turning in a bunch of so-called exnays—illegals trying to pass themselves off as legitimate citizens. Just what I said before. Except all the supposed 'exnays' actually *were* legitimate citizens, some of them with very powerful and well-connected families. Just think if the Population Police had fallen for your little ploy . . ."

Nina stopped listening. She had never felt so thick-headed and stupid before in her life. None of this made sense.

"You don't think *I'm* an illegal third child with a fake I.D.?" she asked cautiously.

"Of course not," the man said. "There's no evidence of that. And if you were an exnay yourself, why would you betray your own comrades?"

Nina closed her eyes, afraid the man might see how relieved she was. She felt like turning cartwheels right there in her jail cell. *They don't know!* she wanted to scream. They wouldn't be tracking down Gran and the aunties, and her mother, to arrest all of them for hiding her. No one at Harlow School would get in trouble for harboring a fugitive. The Population Police wouldn't kill Nina for being illegal.

No. They'd just kill her for something she hadn't done. Treason? Turning in exnays?

Nina opened her eyes, gave the hating man her most indignant stare.

"There's been a mistake," she said firmly. "I never tried to turn in any exnays. I never tried to get the Population Police to pay me."

The man whipped out a little notebook and began to write.

"Ah, now you're talking," he murmured. "I knew you'd come to your senses and try to blame Jason, just like he tried to blame you. No honor among thieves, I suppose." He stopped writing but kept his pen poised over the paper. "So, what's your story? You gonna be the poor, innocent little girl who just did what Jason told you? It always helps if you cry during that one."

Nina felt like he'd slapped her.

"No, really," she protested. "I didn't do anything. And Jason didn't, either. I'm sure of it."

"So you can vouch for Jason?" the man asked. "His whereabouts and his actions, every minute of every day?"

"No, but—"

"But what?" The man was smirking now.

"But I *know* Jason. I know he'd never do anything like that."

"Just like you know he'd never betray you," the man said.

"Right! Exactly!" Nina said eagerly.

The man pulled a rectangular plastic case out of the inside pocket of his jacket. He twisted around again and yelled, "Guard?" Moments later the guard appeared and passed a metal box through the bars.

"Ever seen a tape recorder before?" the man asked Nina.

"No," Nina said.

"Well, that's what this is. We can record anything anyone says. On a tape." He held up the plastic case he'd taken out of his pocket. He slipped the tape into the recorder. "And once we've recorded something, we can play it back as many times as we want." He pushed a button.

Nina heard a whirring sound, then a voice. The tape was a little crackly and hard to hear, like TV on brownout days. But Nina still recognized the voice: Jason's. She leaned forward eagerly, as if Jason were really there and she could throw herself in his arms.

"And Nina said to me, 'Did you ever see those commercials on TV? About third kids and how the Population Police want to hunt them down?' She said, 'I bet they'd pay good money if we turned somebody in.' And I said, 'I don't know any third kids.' And she laughed and said, 'So what? All we have to do is pretend. We can turn in anybody we want. And we'll get a reward.' And I said, 'But that's *lying!* That's wrong! We can't do that.' But then she made me—you know how girls are."

Nina reached out and grabbed the tape recorder. She hurled it at the opposite wall as hard as she could. It cracked hitting the concrete; the tape crashed out when it fell to the floor. Nina strained to reach for the tape because she wanted to destroy it, too. But the man was quicker than she was. His hand closed around the tape as Nina's handcuffs bit into her wrists, holding her back. He put the tape back in his pocket.

"Now, now," he said. "What a temper." He pulled his notebook out again. "So can I put you on record as saying exactly what Jason said, only with the names reversed? 'And *Jason* said to me, "I bet they'd pay good money if we turned somebody in." . . . And I said, "But that's *lying!* It's wrong! We can't do that!" ' " He made his imitation of Nina's voice prissy and falsetto and incredibly childish.

Nina didn't answer. She turned her face toward the wall so the man couldn't see that she was crying. Vaguely a thought flickered in her mind, *This isn't a nightmare. Even nightmares are never this bad.*

"Do I take your silence for agreement?" the man goaded her. "But what are you agreeing to? That you want to betray this Jason you knew so well, the way he betrayed you? Or that what he said was right, and you're to blame for everything? Which is it?"

Nina forced herself to look back at the man.

"I," she said fiercely, "will never agree with anything you say."

"Hmm," the man said. "That's interesting. Because I was about to make you an offer that could save your life. But it appears you're not in the greatest of moods at the moment. Guess my offer will have to wait."

He stood up and took his chair and the pieces of the broken tape recorder and let himself out of her cell. Nina kept her head turned away from him so she could sob facing the wall.

But when Nina was sure he was gone, she looked back and saw that he'd left behind a white handkerchief, neatly folded, perfectly pressed. Nina grabbed the handkerchief and crumpled it into a ball, ready to hurl it at the wall as well. But a handkerchief wouldn't hit with as much satisfying force as the tape recorder had. A handkerchief would only float gently to the ground, like a bird finding a safe perch.

Nina looked around to make sure no one was watching, then loudly blew her nose.

CHAPTER FIVE

Nina ate the bread, too. She was disgusted with herself, that she could gobble up every crumb and eat the wormy apple down to its seeds. She should be pining for Jason, sobbing endlessly like some poor spurned heroine in one of Aunty Zenka's books. But Nina wasn't heartbroken anymore. She was mad. The food just gave her more energy for fury.

"I was a Ninny Idiot," she muttered to herself. "I deserve my name."

How could he? How could Jason have stood there in the moonlight, night after night, gazing into her eyes so lovingly, then turn around and do this? Had he been planning to betray her even a month ago, the first time he'd whispered in her ear, "Why don't we let the others go on back? We still have a few more minutes, just for us"? And then he'd held her hand and nuzzled her neck, and Nina had felt weak clear down to her toes. Even now she could still feel the sensation of his hand against hers, the pressure of his lips on hers. She had relived every kiss, every touch, so many times. Her ears could still bring back the sound of his voice, whispering, "I love you."

But he hadn't loved her. He'd told the Population Police she'd done something evil, and they were going to kill her for it.

Nina spit out an apple seed with such force that it bounced across the floor.

She'd made a total fool of herself over Jason. She could remember all those meetings they'd held out in the woods, when she'd stared at him adoringly and said stupid things. Flirting. She could remember one time when a new boy, Lee Grant, had started coming outside, too. Jason was telling Lee about the rally that Jen Talbot had held, to demonstrate for the rights of third children. And Nina hadn't contributed a thing to the conversation except to echo Jason, "The rally . . ." She wasn't capable of saying anything intelligent, because she wasn't really listening to the conversation, just watching the dim light on Jason's face, admiring his strong profile. Studying the perfect slope of his nose.

Idiotic.

Even before that, before the first time she and Jason kissed, she'd flirted in a different way, acting big, making fun of males. "Well, isn't that just like a boy!" she'd said probably a hundred times, with a simpering, stupid look on her face. She'd felt like she was acting in one of Aunty Zenka's TV dramas. All she needed was a ball gown and one of those dainty little fold-up fans to wave in front of her face whenever she said something particularly precious.

Ridiculous. That's how she'd really looked—ridiculous. How had she forgotten? She was a gawky thirteen-year-old with thin braids hanging down on either side of her face. Even if she'd had the ball gown and the fold-up fan, they would only have made her look sillier.

No wonder Jason had betrayed her. No wonder Sally and Bonner had inched away from her in the woods, like they didn't want to be seen with her.

Nina wanted to cry again, but the tears didn't come. Her heart felt like a rock inside her chest. Everything around her was cold and hard and merciless: the concrete walls, the cement floor, the iron bars of her door. She had thought she could wrap herself in her memories of being loved—by Jason, by her friends at Harlow, by Gran and the aunties. But Jason's love was fake. Her friends hadn't defended her. And Gran and the aunties seemed so far away and long ago that it seemed like it was some other little girl they had loved. Some little Elodie that Nina could barely remember.

Nina fell asleep, dry-eyed and hard-hearted, just one more cold thing in the jail.

CHAPTER SIX

"Here's the deal," the man said.

It was the middle of the night again, Nina thought, blinking stupidly and trying to wake up. The overhead light was blinding again. She felt dizzy from lack of food. Two crusts of bread and one small apple—in what, a day and a half?—did almost nothing to stave off hunger.

"We think you can be useful to us," the man was saying smoothly. He was holding out his hand to her. Nina blinked a few more times and made her eyes focus. What the man had in his hand was too incredible to be believed: a sandwich. And it wasn't black bread and moldy cheese, the kind of sandwich Nina was used to, but a towering bun, thick and golden brown, with pale pink curls of—was that ham?—*ham* overflowing the sides. Nina had seen such a thing only on TV, on the forbidden channels that showed life before the famines.

"Here. Take it," the man said, waving the sandwich carelessly before Nina's eyes.

Nina had half the sandwich shoved in her mouth before she was even conscious of reaching for it.

"I see nobody ever bothered to teach you manners," the man said in disgust.

Nina ignored him. The sandwich was divine. The bun was light and airy and hid a slice of pungent cheese along with the ham. There were other flavors, too—the words from an ancient commercial flowed through Nina's mind: "Lettuce, tomato, pickle, onion . . ." Nina wasn't sure if that was actually what she was eating, but the sandwich was wonderful, absolutely perfect. She slowed down her chewing, just to savor it longer.

"That's better," the man said huffily. Nina had almost forgotten he was there. He handed her a bottle to drink from, and the liquid it contained was delicious, too, sweet and lemony. Nina drank deeply, thinking of nothing but her thirst.

When the sandwich was gone and the bottle was empty, she finally looked back at the man.

"A . . . a deal?" she said hesitantly.

"By law, we could have executed you the day we arrested you," the man said. "But sometimes even the Population Police can benefit from ignoring certain aspects of the law."

Nina waited, frozen in her spot.

"Oh, not that we would *break* the law," the man said. "Given the importance of our mission, there are loopholes written specifically for us. Say we have a criminal in front of us who might be rejuvenated to serve our needs. What purpose is there in executing her?"

"What," Nina asked through clenched teeth, "do you want me to do?"

The man shrugged. "Nothing that you and your buddy Jason weren't pretending to do anyway."

The words flew out of Nina's mouth before she could stop them: "Would Jason help me?"

"Jason, alas, did not seem as useful as you," the man said with an even more careless shrug.

"So he's—"

"Dead? Of course," the man said. "Swift and efficient justice, that's our motto."

Nina felt like everything was falling apart inside her. Her lips trembled.

"Now, now," the man said. "Don't give me any of that fake grief. He betrayed you, remember? Didn't hesitate an instant to stab you in the back when he thought it would save his own neck. Which it didn't, naturally. But I guess someone who would betray his own country wouldn't care in the least about betraying a mere girl."

Nina tried not to listen, but it was impossible. Jason had betrayed her. She remembered his voice on the tape, cold and calculating. She felt her anger coming back, and it was a relief, something to hold on to.

"Why did you think I could be useful and not him?" she asked, doing her best to hold her voice steady.

"I dunno. Maybe I can't see a little girl with braids as a hardened criminal," the man said carelessly. "Maybe I think the ones you need to trick would be more likely to trust a girl. Maybe I just didn't like Jason."

Nina longed to defend Jason, to yell and scream at this man that he was a fine one to be calling Jason unlikable. But it was impossible to defend Jason. Surely he had known that betraying Nina would lead to her death. *Why* had he done it? Why had he tried to trick the Population Police himself?

Nina didn't have time to lose herself in such questions. The man was talking again, explaining what he meant for her to do.

"We have a group of illegals that we've arrested," he said. "Shadow children with fake I.D.'s—"

"I thought you said that was impossible. Shadow children can't get fake I.D.'s," Nina interrupted.

"Well, not *good* ones. Not ones that would fool anyone in authority," the man said. "That's why these kids got caught. I wouldn't be surprised if these kids made the fake I.D.'s themselves. But they're not talking. I have a duty, to the Population Police, to find out who made those I.D.'s, if there's anyone else involved in this evil. And we need to know who's been harboring these illegal children all these years. They were all found out in the street, and they refuse to reveal their parents' names or addresses. You see our dilemma? If we execute the children immediately, other criminals—the ones who hid them, the ones who made their I.D.'s—will never be caught. But if we put you in the same prison cell as these kids, and you get them to trust you and tell you the truth, then you can tell me, and we can get rid of all the criminals. And society's needs will be served. Do you understand?"

Nina understood, all right. That was why she was shivering violently. Even her braids were shaking.

"And if I refuse?" she asked. Her voice shook, too.

The man raised his eyebrows. "You would dare even to think of that as an option?" he thundered. "If you refuse, you join your wonderful friend Jason. You die."

The sandwich that had tasted so good only a few minutes ago was now churning in Nina's stomach. How could she possibly agree to do what the man was asking of her?

But how could she *not* agree, and let them kill her?

Jason had betrayed her. Her friends had not defended her. It was the way of the world to look out only for yourself.

"Why would any of these shadow children trust me, anyway?" Nina asked.

"Because," the man said, "we'll make them think you're an exnay, too. Surely you can act the part."

Oh, yes. I can do that, Nina thought. *But can I live with myself if I get these kids to trust me, and then I betray them?*

The man was already standing up, brushing crumbs off his pants.

"So, it's settled," he said, as though the conversation was over and Nina had agreed to help. "We'll move you into their cell in the morning."

He turned around and walked slowly toward the door.

It seemed to take him a good five minutes to get his key out, put it in the lock, turn the key so the door sprang open. Nina kept telling herself to call out to him, *Wait! I won't do it! I'd rather die than work for the Population Police! I* am *an exnay! My name is Elodie and I'm proud of it. . . .* But Nina couldn't get her mouth to open, her tongue to move.

And then the man was out the door. He flipped a switch and Nina's cell was plunged into darkness again. She heard his footsteps echo down the hall, a lonely sound in the bleak prison.

I belong here now, Nina thought. *I am a betrayer. I am evil.*

CHAPTER SEVEN

By morning Nina was thinking about a fairy tale. But this time it wasn't one about a beautiful princess falling in love with a handsome prince. It was "Rumpelstiltskin."

I'm like the miller's daughter, Nina told herself. *The king told her she had to spin straw into gold or die. Given that choice, of course she didn't speak up and say, "Oops, sorry, I can't do it. Kill me." I'm not going to say that, either.* But the miller's daughter wasn't supposed to hurt anyone else. She was just supposed to do something impossible, not wrong.

What Nina was going to do was definitely wrong.

Maybe these other kids will be horrible and nasty, and I'll be glad to betray them, Nina thought. *Maybe they deserve it.*

She couldn't make herself believe that.

Nina was still sitting wide awake in the dark when she heard the door of her jail cell scrape open. A guard came over and yanked on her arm.

"Come on with you," he snarled.

"The handcuffs—I'm chained," Nina protested. "I'm chained to the wall."

The guard swore and kicked her in the stomach. Nina doubled over in pain. *This* was how the Population Police treated people who worked for them?

The guard stalked out of the jail cell and came back moments later with a key. He unlocked the chains on the wall, then jerked Nina to her feet. Nina hadn't stood in two days. Her legs felt stiff and useless beneath her.

"Come *on*!" the guard commanded, pulling on her arm.

Nina stumbled after him. They went down stairs and through long corridors, past dozens of barred doors. Nina wanted to peek in some of them, but it was too dark, and the guard was rushing her too fast. They descended a final set of stairs, and the air got clammier. Nina tripped and fell, and her bare knee touched standing water before she could right herself. She ran her fingers along the stone wall, and it was moist, too.

They were in the basement. Maybe it was even a cave.

They reached yet another door—this one solid wood—and the guard gripped her arm tighter. With his free hand he unlocked the door, then propelled her forward.

"And if you make any more trouble, you'll get even worse!" he yelled as he released his grip on her arm. Nina flew forward, landing in a heap. The door slammed shut behind her.

"Hello?" Nina called tentatively. She peered into the darkness around her but couldn't make out anything. For all she knew, the walls could be inches from her nose, or miles away. "Hello?" she called again. "Is anyone there?"

There was a rustling off to her right. Nina wondered if it was just rats or mice, and this was all a cruel trick. But in the next second a match flared in the darkness, and someone whispered, "No, I've got it. . . ."

And then a candle glowed. In the dim light Nina could make out two—no, three—faces. These were the kids Nina was supposed to betray. In horror she cried out, "Are any of you older than five?"

CHAPTER EIGHT

All three faces stared resentfully back at Nina. She had never seen such filthy, ragged children in all her life. After two days in prison—with her dress torn and blood-soaked, her face streaked with tears and dirt, her braid ties lost—Nina knew she wasn't exactly a fashion plate herself. But these kids looked—and smelled, come to think of it—like they'd been born in one of Aunty Lystra's precious garbage dumps. They had dirt caked on their cheeks. They had smears of who knows what dribbled down their patched, baggy clothes. Their matted hair hung in ragged clumps into their eyes. It was impossible to tell if they were boys or girls. Nina wouldn't even have been surprised to discover that they were neither, but some sort of strange humanlike animal she'd never heard of.

Then they started talking.

"We're *all* older than five," the one in the middle said. "We're just small for our ages."

The smallest one nodded vigorously. "Matthias is ten, Percy is nine, and I'm six."

"And what's your name?" Nina asked gently.

"Alia," the child answered.

Alia. So the littlest one was a girl. *How can I betray a little girl?* Nina asked herself. When Nina was six, her aunties had taken turns holding her on their lap, teaching her to read. Gran herself was in charge of math lessons, and Aunty Rhoda taught her how to spell. Nina could still remember how it felt to snuggle so cozily in an aunty's lap, in the big armchair, with a book balanced on her knees. No matter how cold it got in their apartment, Nina always felt warm, when she was six.

And this six-year-old girl was huddled in a damp jail cell, waiting to die.

"If you don't mind," the biggest one—Matthias?—asked, "I think we'll put out the candle now. We only have the one. But we wanted to get a good look at you."

"Oh, go ahead," Nina said, though she longed for light. Two days in darkness had been much too long.

"My turn!" Alia said joyfully. She leaned over and blew. The flame vanished. Nina longed for it to come back.

But in the darkness I can trick them more easily. They won't be able to tell from my face when I am lying.

Was Nina going to lie to them? She couldn't decide.

"So. Who are you?" an unfamiliar voice—Percy's?—asked in the darkness.

And Nina was already lost. Which name should she say? Which names had they told her—real or fake? She had trouble imagining anyone wanting to name their kid Percy. So they were probably still pretending to be the people their fake I.D.'s said they were.

"You can call me Nina," she said cagily. "But my real name is—"

"No! Don't say it!" Alia screamed.

"We think they might be listening," Matthias explained in a whisper.

"So what?" Nina said recklessly. "They're going to kill us anyway."

Somehow Nina could feel the shocked silence on the other side of the room. Even in the dark she could picture those three grimy faces agape with horror.

"No, they're not," Alia said. "They're going to find out we're innocent, and then they're going to release us."

Alia's voice was buoyant with hope, calm and confident. Did she really believe what she was saying? Was she that stupid? Just from the way the three kids had huddled together, in the brief moments that the candle had been lit, Nina could tell that Matthias and Percy watched out for Alia. Maybe the boys, not wanting a hysterical six-year-old on their hands, had filled her head with lies: "Everything's okay. They won't hurt us. We'll get out soon."

Or was Alia acting, for the sake of the Population Police they thought were listening? Maybe one of the boys had told Alia, "Act like you think we're innocent, and maybe they'll believe it." But could a six-year-old act so convincingly?

Anyway, how could they possibly think the Population

Police were listening? (Or *know*—if Nina told the Population Police everything, wasn't it like they were listening through Nina's ears?)

Nina rubbed her forehead. Everything was a muddle. How could she ever get these kids to trust her and spill all their secrets now? Did she really want them to tell her all their secrets?

I could find out their secrets and just not tell the Population Police, she told herself.

"How long have you been here?" she asked, trying to keep her voice casual, like she didn't really care but didn't have anything else to do but ask questions.

Nobody answered right away. Nina thought maybe they were whispering together on the other side of the room. Then Percy spoke up.

"We don't really know. It's hard to tell day from night down here."

"They've only brought us food three times," Alia said helpfully.

"How were you arrested?" Nina asked.

Again, it was a while before anyone answered. Nina wished so badly that she could see them.

"We were standing in line to buy cabbage. All three of us," Matthias finally said. "The Population Police came through the market, checking I.D.'s. They said ours were fake. So they arrested us—"

"But they're not fake!" Alia interrupted. "They're real, and the Population Police should know that. DO YOU

HEAR ME?" Alia's voice was directed not at Nina, but at the door. Her words echoed so loudly, Nina could barely hear the two boys shushing her.

Nina decided to pretend she didn't notice.

"Why haven't your parents come to get you out?" Nina asked.

"Don't got any parents," Alia said.

Nina noticed the way she'd said that—"Don't got any,"—not "Our parents are dead," or "We live with our grandparents," or "It'd be our aunt coming for us."

"Who takes care of you?" Nina asked cautiously.

"We take care of ourselves," Alia said hotly.

And this time Nina was sure the boys were whispering to Alia, telling her not to say anything else. A miserable lump filled Nina's throat. Filthy as they were, at least those three kids had one another. Nina wanted someone to huddle with, too. *If Jason were here—*

No, not Jason. He was dead now, and anyway, he had betrayed her. How could she forget? Remembering his hugs made her skin crawl; thinking about his kisses made her wish she'd punched him in the nose instead of kissing back. Why hadn't she challenged him: "You keep saying we ought to do something about third children's rights, something like the famous Jen Talbot's rally. So why don't we?" Nina could have exposed him as a fake, right then and there. She could have been a hero, like Jen.

Instead, she was about to become a traitor.

CHAPTER NINE

Nina fell into a miserable sleep because that was the only way to escape. Let the other three whisper together all they wanted.

She woke when a light flashed over her—someone was shining a flashlight in through the open door.

"Nina Idi," a bored voice called.

Nina stumbled to her feet. She glanced around and saw that the other three had fallen asleep as well, in one giant heap. Alia was cuddled in Matthias's lap; Matthias's head was on Percy's shoulder. The light didn't seem to awaken any of them. Alia turned so her face was against Matthias's leg instead of his arm. But her eyes stayed shut.

Nina squinted back toward the light. The person holding it lowered it toward the floor, and Nina could see better without the glare directly in her eyes. It was a guard behind the light, in the shadows.

"Come on now," he said irritably.

Nina thought it might be the same guard as before, but it was hard to tell. Maybe all the guards looked and sounded alike, so grim in their dark uniforms. Nina took a step toward the door, her chains clanking against the stone floor. She turned around, and all three of the other kids were wide awake now.

Nina hated the sight of all those terrified, round eyes.

"You're wanted for questioning," the guard said.

Nina took another step forward, but she watched the other kids exchanging glances. *As soon as I'm gone,* she thought bitterly, *Matthias is going to tell Alia, "See, that's why we can't tell her anything. She's not trustworthy."* Nina would have liked it if even one of the kids had mouthed a "Good luck" at her or flashed her a look of pity. But they all sat as still and silent as statues.

The guard grabbed Nina's arm and pulled her on out the door. But once the door was shut and they were down the hall a bit, the guard bent over and unlocked the chains from her ankles. When he straightened up, he took the cuffs off her wrists.

"You're setting me free?" Nina asked in disbelief.

The man snorted. "Are you crazy?"

But he let her walk on her own, beside him, down the rest of the hall and up the stairs. He turned to the left at the top of the stairs and unlocked a metal door. On the other side of the door there was carpet and soft light and cream-colored walls. It seemed like a different universe than the rest of the prison. It seemed like a different universe than any place she'd ever been. Harlow School for Girls had been nice, especially compared with Gran's apartment. But there had still been cracks in the plaster walls, scuff marks on the tile floor. Here Nina couldn't see so much as a tuft of carpet that wasn't perfect.

The guard must have noticed her awestruck stares, because he snorted again. "Officers' suites," he explained. "Nothing but the best for the top brass."

He led her into a room with a long wooden table, beautifully carved with grapes and apples and other designs Nina couldn't even identify. Nina sat down in a chair, and it was a kind she would have expected the president to use.

"Your interrogator will be here shortly," the guard said, and left.

Nina kept gazing around, blinking in amazement. On each wall portraits hung in elegant gold frames. And at the front of the room two windows stared back at Nina like giant eyes.

Nina didn't know much about windows. Harlow hadn't had any, for some strange reason. And in the apartment with Gran and the aunties they'd had to keep the blinds pulled all the time, for fear that someone outside might see in and get a glimpse of Nina, then report her to the Population Police. ("We're not missing anything, believe me," Aunty Zenka had assured Nina once. "Those windows just look out on an alley and a trash Dumpster. You've done us a favor, actually. How much better it is to look at those blinds and pretend that beautiful scenes lie just beyond—flowing rivers and glorious mountains, rose gardens and towering forests. . . . That's what *I* prefer to think is out there.")

But being seen presented no danger to Nina now. The Population Police had already caught her. Nothing worse could happen. Daringly, she stood up and walked over to one of the windows. Shrubs curled against the glass on the other side. It was bright daylight—something Nina had never seen for real, since it had been raining the day she traveled to Harlow and the day she left it. The sky was a deep, beautiful blue that made something ache in Nina's chest. Wispy white clouds sailed high overhead. And beyond the row of shrubs an expanse of grass sloped down to a lake and, just at the horizon's edge, a small woods.

It was a scene worthy of Aunty Zenka's imagination.

"Enjoying the view?" a voice said behind Nina.

Nina gasped and turned—it was the hating man. She stepped back from the window.

But the man didn't seem upset. He stepped forward and looked out, too.

"Not exactly what you'd expect near a prison, huh?" he mused. Nina wondered if he was just talking to himself. "You'd think, with a prison, there'd be high fences, lots of barbed wire, guards patrolling with guns. . . . And there are, back there, where all the prisoners are. But for this section, well, we officers like to see beauty occasionally. So much of our work is . . . brutal and ugly. You know?"

Nina didn't know if she was supposed to answer or not. After a moment the hating man moved away from the window. "Thank you," he said over his shoulder. He turned back to Nina. "Shall we dine?" he asked her.

Nina saw that while she'd been staring out the window, the guard had silently placed a tray on the table—a tray containing a feast. Roast chicken, platters of potatoes and peas, a basket of airy rolls . . . The man pulled out a chair for Nina. Nina remembered suddenly how grimy she looked—not at all the sort of person who should have a chair pulled out for her. Self-consciously she pushed hair out of her eyes.

"Now, now," the man said. "I'm sure you're longing for a good, long shower, but we do need to keep you in character."

Nina sat down. As if in a dream, she reached for a roll, ate the chicken the man placed on her plate, spooned peas into her mouth, swallowed rich, creamy milk. "This," she heard herself say, "is the best meal I've ever had."

"Well, there are perks to assisting the Population Police," the man replied with a chuckle.

Nina stopped eating.

"Full?" the man said.

"Um, kind of," Nina said, though it wasn't true. Nina could have eaten another huge serving of everything.

"Just a minute," the man said. He stood up and walked toward the door, and seemed to be conferring with the guard about something. Nina stared at the basket of rolls in front of her. The image of Alia's thin, hungry face swam before her eyes. She remembered Alia saying, bravely, "They've only brought us food three times." The man wasn't looking. What would it hurt if Nina swiped just a roll for Alia? She could grab three, even, one for each kid, and hide them in the sleeve of her dress. Nobody would know.

Nina remembered the way the three kids had stared at her when the guard came for her. She remembered how they hadn't said a single word of comfort or encouragement.

She didn't reach for a roll.

Moments later the guard came in and took all the food away. The hating man settled into his chair across from Nina. He leaned back and put his feet on the table.

"Well," he said casually. "I understand that you haven't exactly been winning friends and influencing people. I'd wager that you don't have a single thing to tell me."

"You've been listening!" Nina accused.

The man gave a little snort of amusement. "Now, now. Mighty paranoid, aren't we? Of course we haven't been listening. That's what *you're* in there for. I'm just interpreting body language. Mack—that's the guard; you weren't properly introduced, were you?—Mack tells me that when he came to get you, you were sleeping on one side of the cell, and the other three were huddled together as far from you as possible. Doesn't exactly sound like you've all been palling around together."

"They're all friends together," Nina protested. "They knew one another before they were arrested. I'm just a stranger to them."

"Well, get unstrange, then," the man said. "Don't you want to live?"

Nina gulped.

"They're hungry and cold and terrified. They don't *feel* like talking," Nina said. Even to her own ears she sounded like a whiny child. "And they do think you are listening. They won't talk about . . . certain things because they think the Population Police can hear everything. It's hopeless!"

The man clicked his tongue in disapproval.

"I thought you were smarter than that," he said, shaking his head. "You have to make them tell you things. You work for the Population Police now. Act like it!"

CHAPTER TEN

Nina stumbled back into her jail cell to find the other three huddled around a burning candle.

"Alia got scared," Matthias explained. "She thought you might have been . . . you know."

Nina glanced over her shoulder, afraid that the guard might see the candle and take it away. But he was already slamming the door, locking it. He hadn't even looked into the cell.

"You were . . . worried about me?" Nina asked.

Matthias only shrugged, but Alia nodded, her eyes huge and solemn in her skinny face. Nina suddenly felt horrible that she hadn't snatched any rolls for the other kids.

"What did they want?" Percy asked.

"They just asked some questions."

"They did that to us, too, when we first came," Alia said. "They took us away, one at a time. But none of us said anything dangerous. Sa—I mean, we knew just what to say."

Nina heard that one slip of the tongue, "Sa—," and because the candle was still burning, she saw Matthias dig his elbow into Alia's side. To warn her? To silence her?

What had she almost said? "Sa—" Was it the beginning of someone's name?

Nina struggled to keep from showing the others how curious she was about that one little syllable, "Sa—".

"How did you know what to say, and what not to say?" Nina asked, hoping to make it sound like she just wanted to be able to avoid problems herself. "Did someone tell you?"

"Oh, we just knew," Alia said. "We're all pretty smart. Like, say you're a shadow child. Just pretend. If you're a shadow child, you're safe as long as you never ever tell the Population Police your real name."

"Of course," Nina said. "If I were a shadow child, and I had a fake I.D., I sure wouldn't tell anybody my real name. Besides my family, I mean."

But she had. She could remember one night when Jason had kissed her under the trees. He'd whispered in her ear, "You're so beautiful, and I don't even know who you really are. . . ." And the words had slipped out: "Elodie . . . I'm Elodie. . . ." It was her gift to him.

And look what he had done with it.

"Did you tell the Population Police anything about us?" Percy was asking. His question brought Nina back to the present, back to the cold, dripping jail cell and the six eyes staring at her and the horrible choice she was going to have to make.

"Just that you were hungry and cold down here," Nina said. It really wasn't even a lie. "And I told the man who was asking questions that you all thought they were listening to everything we said down here. He laughed and said that was ridiculous."

"Why did you say that?" Matthias asked furiously. "If they know we know, now we can't say anything to trick them."

Nina was getting confused, but she thought she knew what he meant.

"Well, it hasn't done any good so far, has it?" she challenged. "You're still stuck down here, and they haven't fed you, and they haven't even given you soap to wash your face!"

"They haven't killed us, either," Alia said softly. Nina stared at the younger girl. *When I was six, I wouldn't have known to say something like that,* she thought. *I was still a baby, playing with dolls and dressing up in the aunties' old clothes, pretending to be a princess. And I had four old ladies treating me like a princess.*

"I'm sorry," Nina said. "I didn't mean to do anything wrong."

But she'd let the hating man think she was going to spy for him. She'd eaten his food, and that was like . . . like taking blood money or something. She hadn't refused anything. She hadn't screamed and hollered and told him that the Population Police were wrong. She hadn't demanded that he set Matthias and Percy and Alia—and herself—free.

Nina bent her head down, too ashamed to look at the others.

A scraping sound behind her saved her from having to say anything else.

"Food!" Alia said delightedly.

The guard was opening the door. He tossed in a dark bundle, then shut the door and retreated.

Alia reached the bundle first. She grabbed it up and took it over to the boys. Matthias held the candle so they could all see in.

"Ooh, Nina, look!" Alia squealed. "There's one, two, three, four, five . . . eight slices of bread! They've never brought more than six before!"

"There's one more of us now, silly," Percy said. "We still get two each."

"Oh," Alia said.

Nina moved over with the other kids, feeling like she'd crossed some invisible line. She squatted down with them and peered into the bag. It held the same kind of hard black bread she'd had for her first meal in prison. There wasn't even any butter or apples to go with it. After her feast with the hating man she couldn't pretend to want this bread.

"You know what?" she said with studied casualness. "I'm not really hungry. Why don't you all take my slices, too?"

They all stared at her.

"Are you sure?" Alia asked. "I don't think they feed us every day."

"That's okay. You take it," Nina said.

They didn't need any extra urging. In seconds the three kids had gobbled up all the bread. Nina did notice, though, that Matthias had a strange way of dividing up Nina's share of the food: Alia got a whole slice, and Matthias and Percy split the other one. Nina's full stomach ached, watching the others eat so hungrily.

When they were done, they searched for any dropped crumbs and ate those as well. Nina hovered beside them, pretending to look for crumbs, too. Then they all sat back, happily sated. Nina sat down beside Alia, and Alia leaned over and gave her a big hug.

"Thanks, Nina. I hope you don't get hungry later. I think that was the best meal I ever had."

Nina could have brought Alia fresh, beautiful rolls, but she hadn't. Instead, she'd let the little girl have old, moldy, practically inedible black bread just because Nina herself was too full of the Population Police's fine meal to pretend to want it. And now Alia was thanking her.

Nina felt guiltier than ever.

CHAPTER ELEVEN

Days passed. Nina had no idea how many, because nothing happened with any regularity. Sometimes the guard brought food; sometimes the guard pulled one of them out for questioning. Sometimes Matthias decided they could light the candle for a few minutes—but only for Alia, only when he thought she needed it.

Nobody knew when any of those things would happen.

Other than that, they could measure their time in the prison-cave only by how many times they got sleepy or thirsty or needed to go to the bathroom.

None of those needs were easily satisfied.

Their "bathroom" was just a corner of the cave they all avoided as much as they could. It stank mightily.

They had no bedding at all, not a single pillow or blanket. Sleeping on wet rock only left Nina damp and stiff and more tired than ever.

And when they were thirsty, they had to go to the dampest part of the cave and lick the wall. The guard never brought water. Matthias got the idea to keep one of the cloth bags the food had come in, in order to soak up as much water as possible. (He told the guard they'd dropped the bag over in the bathroom corner. "He won't come in here and check," he argued in a barely audible whisper. And he was right.) Matthias put the bag at the bottom of the damp wall, where the water dripped constantly. When the bag was saturated, he carefully squeezed the water from the wet cloth into Alia's waiting mouth, and then Percy's, and then a few precious drops into Nina's. Nina choked and spit it out.

"Yu-uck!" she screamed.

"What?" Alia asked.

"It tastes terrible," Nina complained. The water was unpleasant enough licked straight from the wall—it tasted like rock and sulfur and, distantly, some kind of chemical Nina couldn't identify. But from the cloth bag the water tasted like rock and moldy bread and old, rotting, dirty bag. Maybe even somebody else's vomit as well.

"It's water," Matthias said. "It'll keep us alive."

Nina didn't say anything else. But after that, she went back to getting her water straight from the wall, a drop or two at a time, and let the others squeeze all the water from the cloth for themselves.

Nina suspected that the other three kids had had a much rougher life than she before they were captured by the Population Police. They didn't seem to mind the darkness like she did; they didn't seem to mind the lack of food. They didn't complain about the stench of the bathroom corner. (Well, they all smelled bad themselves anyway. So did Nina.)

Nina tried as much as possible to sit close to the other kids—for body warmth and to keep the guard from tattling on her again. And maybe to learn something. But several times she woke up from a deep sleep and found that they'd moved to another side of the room and were whispering together.

"There was a draft over there," Alia would say. "We got cold, but you looked comfortable. We didn't want to wake you."

It sounded so innocent. Maybe it was innocent. But it still made Nina mad.

I will betray them, she'd think. *That'll show them. And I won't care at all.*

That was when she'd moan something like, "Oh, I miss my family so bad. Who do you miss?"

Even Alia wouldn't answer a question like that.

And later, facing the hating man, Nina would be glad for the other kids' silence. Because, with his piercing blue eyes glaring at her, she knew she wouldn't be able to keep any secrets. She felt like he knew she really was an exnay. She felt like, if he asked, she'd be forced to tell him Gran's full name and address. Whether she wanted to or not, she'd describe every single one of her aunties down to their last gray hair, and give their civil service ranks and departments.

Fortunately, he never asked about who had hidden her.

He just asked about Alia, about Percy, about Matthias.

"Give me more time," Nina would beg. "I don't know them yet." (Though, secretly, Nina thought she could spend centuries in the prison-cave with them and still not know anything about them. Percy was like a rock, hard and unyielding, revealing nothing. Matthias was no more talkative than a tree. Even Alia, who looked like the weak spot on their team of three, was quiet more and more, polite and nothing else.)

"Time? You've been in there for days," the hating man ranted back during one interrogation session in the middle of the night. "How long does it take to say, 'My parents are so-and-so. What are your parents' names?' "

For one terrifying instant Nina thought he really was asking her her parents' names. Against her will her lips began to pucker together to form the first syllable of her mother's name. *Rita. My mother's name is Rita. My father's name is Lou. Gran's name is Ethel. And I am . . .*

Nina bit down hard, trapping all those words in her mouth. The hating man didn't seem to notice. He was pacing, facing away from her. He continued fuming.

"Even first names would help. Even initials. You've got to give me something."

He hadn't been asking her her parents' names. He'd merely been telling her the question she was supposed to ask the others. Nina's heart pounded out a panicky rhythm that made it hard for her to think.

What if . . . what if he doesn't care about my parents'

names because he already knows them? What if he already knows about Gran and the aunties? Is that why he never asks?

Nina frantically tried to remember if she'd ever breathed a word about any of her family to Jason. She hadn't, had she? Talking to Jason, she'd wanted to seem exotic and desirable. A grandmother and a bunch of old-maid aunts didn't really fit that image.

The hating man was done pacing. He whirled on his heel, put his face right up against Nina's. They were eye to eye, nose to nose.

"You cannot play around with the Population Police, little girl," he said. "That's how people die."

Nina quivered.

The man stalked out and slammed the door behind him.

Nina sat alone, terrified, in the luxurious interrogation room. The table in front of her was loaded down with bowls of food. She'd been eating ravenously during their conversation. Perhaps because it was the middle of the night, instead of midday, the foods were snacks, not a real meal, mostly things Nina had never tasted before: popcorn, peanuts in their salty shells, orange cheese crackers, raisins in delicate little boxes. Nina was still starving—she was always starving, she couldn't think of a single time in her entire life when she'd had her belly completely full. But she couldn't bring herself to eat another bite, not with the hating man's threat echoing in her ears. Still, she found herself reaching out for the bowl of peanuts. She watched her own hands lift the bowl and pour its contents down the front of her dress, making a bag of her bodice. She cinched her belt tighter, holding the peanuts in at her waist. She'd barely finished when the guard opened the door.

"He's done with you early, I hear," the guard growled. "Back to the cell with you."

Nina stood slowly. None of the peanuts fell out. She crossed her arms and held them tightly at her waist, keeping the belt in place. She took a step, and then another, and nothing happened. The peanut shells tickled, but Nina didn't care.

I'm stealing food from the Population Police! Nina thought. *I'm getting away with it!*

Walking back to her cell, Nina did not feel like a girl who'd nearly betrayed her parents, whose beloved Gran and aunties might be in danger. She did not feel like an illegal child, with no right to live. She did not feel like a lovesick, silly teenager who'd been betrayed by the boy she'd fallen for. She did not feel like a potential traitor to her own kind.

She felt giddy and hopeful, crafty and capable. All because of the rustle of peanut shells under her dress.

CHAPTER TWELVE

Nina kept stealing food.

Invariably, during every meeting with the hating man there came a time when he'd leave the room briefly—to confer with the guard, to go to the bathroom, to get a new pen. And then Nina would grab whatever food was nearest and stuff it down her dress, in her socks, wherever she could. She took apples, oranges, biscuits, raisins. She took dried bananas, unshelled walnuts, cereal boxes, oatmeal bars still in their wrappers. She stole another of the bags the guard brought black bread in, and took to carrying it around with her, tied under her dress, so she could swipe even more food each time.

The problem was, she didn't know what to do with the food she stole.

She was hungry. She could easily have eaten it all herself. But once she was back in her jail cell with the other three, her stomach squeezed together at the thought of eating so much as a crumb of the stolen food. What if they heard her chewing? How could she eat such delicacies while they were starving, right there beside her? (How could she eat any of the Population Police's food when the other three were starving?)

She did think about sharing. That was probably why she'd reached for the bowl of peanuts in the first place, because she felt so guilty about not taking the rolls for Alia. But how could she explain where she'd gotten all that food?

An evil thought crept into her mind one night when the guard shoved her back into her cell and she saw the other three cuddled together. Nina sat down beside them and leaned into Alia, and Alia squirmed away in her sleep, closer to Matthias. The ground was wet and hard, and Nina was freezing. Everything seemed hopeless; Nina didn't care what happened to anyone else as long as *she* got warm, as long as *she* got dry clothes, as long as *she* got out of jail. *I could use the food,* she thought. *Like a bribe. I could tell them they can have as much as they want to eat, as long as they tell me their secrets. No—I'd dole it out, a peanut at a time, a raisin at a time, with every one of my questions. Who's "Sa-"? Where'd you get your I.D.'s? Who else should have been arrested with you?*

Nina didn't do it. She just kept stealing food she couldn't eat, couldn't give away, couldn't use. She felt like she'd been in prison forever and she would stay in prison forever. She saw nothing ahead of her but more nights sleeping in damp, filthy clothes on cold, hard rock, more days trying to overhear the others' whispers, more randomly spaced trips to the hating man's room, where he yelled at her and gave her food she could not eat, only steal.

Then one day he cut her off.

"You have twenty-four hours," the hating man barked at her. "That's it."

Nina stared back at him, her brain struggling to comprehend. She'd practically forgotten that twenty-four hours made a day—that there were things such as numbers and counted-off hours in the world.

"You mean . . . ," she said, more puzzled than terrified.

"If you do not tell me everything I need to know by"—he looked at the watch on his wrist—"by ten-oh-five tomorrow night, you will be executed. You and the three exnays."

Nina waited for the terror to come, but she was too numb. And then she was too distracted. Mack, the guard, was pounding at the door to their meeting room. The hating man opened it, and Mack stumbled in, slumping against the table. Nina saw he still clutched the ring of keys he always used to get her in and out of her cell. His long arms hit the wood hard. Then his fingers released, and the keys went sliding across the table and onto the floor.

"Poi—," Mack gulped. "Poisoned . . ."

The hating man sprang up and grabbed a phone, punching numbers with amazing speed. "Ambulance to the Population Police headquarters immediately!" he demanded. "One of our guards has been poisoned."

He dragged Mack out into the hall, Mack's feet bouncing against the floor. "Stay with me, Mack," the hating man muttered. "They're coming to help you."

"Unnhh," Mack groaned.

Both of them seemed to have forgotten Nina. Nina looked down and saw the guard's key ring on the floor, just to the left of her chair. All the keys stuck out at odd angles. Slowly, carelessly, as if it were nothing more than just another stray peanut shell, Nina bent down and picked up the whole ring.

CHAPTER THIRTEEN

Nina slipped the ring of keys around her left wrist and pushed it up her arm—farther, farther—until the ring stayed in place on its own. The points of the keys bit into her arm, but it wasn't an entirely unpleasant sensation. It woke her up.

I have keys.

I have food.

I have twenty-four hours.

I need a plan.

The hating man strode back into the room. Nina didn't have the slightest idea how long he'd been gone. Maybe she'd been sitting there fingering the keys through her sleeve for hours.

"I can't believe this!" the man fumed. "Mack's—I've got someone else with Mack now. I'll take you back to your cell. Come on! I want to get back here as soon as I can. . . ."

Nina stood up, feeling the full weight of the food bag tied around her waist, the pinch of every individual key around her arm. As slowly as she dared, she circled the table toward the hating man. He grabbed her arm—her right one, fortunately—and pulled.

"Don't know what this world's coming to," the man muttered as they came to the door from the luxurious hallway into the rest of the prison. Nina held her breath. Would he realize now that he needed Mack's keys?

No—he was pulling keys of his own out of his jacket pocket, jamming a key into the lock, jerking the key around, jabbering the whole time. "Mack's a good, honest man, got kids of his own—I don't know why . . ."

They were at another door. The man unlocked this one, too, with barely a pause.

Down the stairs, through another door—the man hustled Nina all the way. Nina was daring to breathe again. Then they reached the door of Nina's cell.

The hating man stopped, stared at his key ring.

"Wouldn't you know it!" he grumbled. "I'm missing this key. I'll have to go back for it."

He glanced around toward the door they'd just come through. The disgust and impatience played over his face so clearly, Nina felt like she could read his mind: *Now I'll have to go all the way back upstairs, take this nasty girl with me, then come back down here into this muck.* Yes, that had to be what he was thinking. He even raised his foot distastefully to look at the mud on the bottom of his polished shoe. *And I don't want to have to think about this useless kid anymore, I just want to go check on poor Mack—*

"Tell you what," the hating man said. "I'm not even going to put you in the cell. I'll just leave you in this hall. There isn't anyone else in this wing right now anyway, and that door will be locked tight. . . ." He spoke as though it were Nina, not he, who might worry that she wouldn't be imprisoned well enough. "The morning guard can put you back in your cell when he comes through on his eight A.M. rounds."

He was already going back through the other door. "Can't be helped," he muttered, and shut the door in Nina's face.

Nina stood beside the solid metal door and put her finger over the keyhole. One of the keys on Mack's key ring fit into that hole. She was sure of it. If the hating man had put her back in her cell, the keys would have done her no good; the door of the prison cell couldn't be unlocked from the inside.

But she had keys to all the doors between her and the interrogation room, with its windows to the outside.

She had keys, she had food—she could escape.

CHAPTER FOURTEEN

Nina blindly poked keys into the keyhole, searching for the right one. The only light in the hallway was a dim, dirty bulb, several yards away, so she had trouble just keeping track of which keys she'd already tried and which keys she hadn't. It was also hard trying to keep the rest of the key ring from banging on the metal door while she was turning each individual key. She was sure she had to work silently. But why? Surely the hating man was already upstairs, hovering over the poisoned Mack. And he'd said there were no other prisoners down here. Except Percy, Matthias, and Alia, of course.

Percy, Matthias, and Alia.

It was strange, but Nina had not thought about them even once since that first moment her fingers closed around the guard's key ring. She'd forgotten they existed. All she'd thought about were the keys, the keyholes, her own life.

Percy, Matthias, and Alia.

Thinking about them now made Nina drop the whole ring of keys. It clattered to the stone floor and slid several inches. The sound seemed to bounce all around in Nina's ears, as though she'd dropped a thousand keys on a thousand floors. She half wished one of the three kids—Percy, Matthias, or Alia—would pound on their cell door, yell out, "Hey! What's going on out there?"

Because then Nina would have to talk to them, have to face them, have to look into their eyes while she decided, *Should I ask them to come with me?*

But none of them pounded on the door, none of them called out to her. She shouldn't have expected them to. If they had even heard the noise of the keys through the heavy wood door, they probably just assumed it was a guard making a little more racket than usual. Whether they heard the noise or not, they would have stayed cowering together in their little corner of the cell. In prison it was foolish to call attention to yourself.

In prison it was foolish to think about anyone but yourself.

Nina still didn't bend over to pick up the keys. Not yet.

Ever since the hating man had told her, days ago, "Here's the deal," she'd been avoiding any decisions. She'd lain down in filth, she'd stumbled along behind the guard, she'd sat with her head bowed while the hating man harangued her. But she hadn't done anything to harm Percy, Matthias, and Alia. She hadn't exactly done anything to help them, either—she'd sat precisely in the middle of a perfectly balanced scale.

But now it was time to tip the scale. She had to choose.

If Nina left on her own, without a single look back,

she'd be sending Percy, Matthias, and Alia to their death. Hadn't the hating man said he was going to kill them all if he didn't get the information he needed by ten o'clock the next night? In her heart of hearts Nina knew that that "if" helped only her—if Percy, Matthias, and Alia were still in their jail cell tomorrow, he'd kill them.

But I don't have that much food, Nina thought. *It'd be harder for four kids to hide out, traveling to safety, than just one. And Alia's so little. She probably can't walk very fast at all, and I need to walk as far as possible tonight, before anyone discovers I'm gone. One way or another, those kids are going to die. Taking them with me would just mean that I die, too.*

Nina thought about Jason betraying her, about all her friends just staring when the Population Police came to arrest her. *Nobody helped me!* she wanted to yell at that small, stubborn part of herself that refused just to pick up the keys and go. But then she thought about Gran, Aunty Zenka, Aunty Lystra, and Aunty Rhoda, four old ladies who could have enjoyed the few small luxuries they could afford on their old-age pensions. They'd kept working instead, at mindless, drudgery-filled jobs, and diapered and coddled a small child in their off hours. She thought about her own mother, a woman she'd barely met, hiding her pregnancy, traveling secretly to Gran's house, sending money whenever she could. It would have been easier for everyone if they'd gotten rid of Nina right from the start.

But it would have been wrong.

Nina sighed, letting out all the damp, unhealthy prison air she'd been breathing. Then she bent down and scooped up the keys. She turned around and walked to a different door, fumbled for a different key. Amazingly, she found this one on the first try. The solid wood door creaked open.

"Alia? Percy? Matthias?" she called. "Come on. Let's get out of here."

CHAPTER FIFTEEN

Six eyes bugged out at Nina. She had thought she'd lost all awareness of time, but she could feel seconds ticking away—useful, possibly lifesaving seconds—while the others stared speechlessly at her.

"Huh?" Percy finally said.

"I stole a lot of food," Nina said. "Then somebody poisoned the guard, and he dropped his keys, and the hating man didn't see me pick them up, and he was in a hurry, so he didn't bring me all the way back to the cell, he just wanted to get back to Mack as soon as possible. Mack's the guard. Anyway, I have the keys, and nobody knows it, so we can escape. Come on!"

Another long pause. They didn't seem to understand.

"Did you poison the guard?" Alia asked in a small voice.

"No—I don't know who poisoned him. I don't care. All that matters is that it made him drop his keys, and now I have them, and I'm running away. And you guys can come, too, if you come *now*."

"Maybe it's a trick," Percy muttered.

"Maybe it's a test," Matthias muttered back. He stood up

and walked over to Nina. "Why should we trust you?" he asked.

Nina's jaw dropped. She'd expected them to be delighted, grateful, eager to leave immediately. She'd never dreamed that they might question her offer.

"Why should you trust me?" she repeated numbly. "Because . . . because you're sitting in this horrible prison cell, licking water off the wall and peeing in a corner. And tomorrow, if you're still here, the Population Police are going to execute you. You don't exactly have tons of choices here. I'm your only chance."

Percy and Alia came to stand beside Matthias, like reinforcements.

"She has a point," Percy whispered to Matthias. "But . . ."

Nina was losing patience. This was entirely backward. They should be pleading with her, not her with them.

"And I'm a nice person," she argued. "Really I am. You don't really know me because I haven't been myself here in prison, because . . ." She couldn't say "because I was trying to decide whether or not to betray you." "Never mind. But you can trust me. I promise."

Percy looked at Alia. Alia looked at Matthias, who looked back at Percy.

"Okay. We're coming," Matthias announced.

"Well, *good,*" Nina said, unable to resist a hint of sarcasm. "Glad that's decided." She turned back toward the other door, rattling the key ring in her hand.

"What's your plan?" Percy asked.

"Plan?" Nina repeated.

"Didn't you say some guard had been poisoned?" Percy asked. "How are you going to avoid all the other guards, who'll be scared and angry and looking for someone to blame?"

"Um—," Nina said.

"And where are we running away to?"

Nina felt stupid. Just as the keys had made her forget Percy, Matthias, and Alia, they'd also made her forget all logic. She couldn't just run away from prison. She had to run *to* someplace else.

She thought about Gran and the aunties', but it was too dangerous. And at Harlow School—everyone there knew she'd been arrested. Nobody would dare to help hide her. She swallowed hard.

"Do you know any place safe?" she asked quietly.

Again the other kids did their three-way look, this time Alia peering at Percy, Percy peering at Matthias, Matthias peering at Alia. It was probably a good thing that most of the time Nina had spent with the other kids had been in darkness, because that look would have driven her crazy.

Maybe it still would.

"We don't know any place safe," Matthias said. "Not anymore."

"Well, this is just great," Nina raged, slumping against the wall. "We have food, we have keys, we have everything we need to escape—except a place to go."

"It's not an easy thing, surviving. Out there," Percy said,

jerking his head toward the metal door, as if the entire world lay just on the other side. "You need food, you need shelter, you need heat—well, not this time of year, but come winter—"

"You need to be safe from other people," Alia chimed in.

"Away from the Population Police, or anyone who might report you to the Population Police," Matthias agreed.

Nina was beginning to regret her decision. The last thing she needed right now was to be lectured by three little kids about how dangerous the world was. Didn't they think she knew that? As if there was any place away from people.

An idea tickled Nina's brain. *Away from people* . . . Like a slide show, her mind flashed on image after image of trees, just trees—a woods going on for miles, between vast yards that led up to two schools without windows. Schools whose students probably never went out into the woods anymore, after Nina and Jason were arrested. . . .

"I think I know a place," Nina said slowly, still thinking.

"Does it have lots of food?" Alia said eagerly.

"No, but . . ." Nina gave the bag at her waist a little tug through the material of her dress. She was being foolish again, though, because the four of them would probably eat all her stolen food before they even got to the woods. And it wasn't like there'd be food lying around in the woods—or would there? Nina remembered the new boy in Jason's group of friends from Hendricks School. He'd called himself Lee Grant, though Jason had told Nina more than once that he was sure that was a fake name. The first time Nina met Lee, he was furious because he'd been making a garden in the woods, and the other kids had trampled on it.

Food grew in gardens. Nina was a city kid, but she knew that much. If Lee Grant could make a garden in the woods, so could Nina and Percy and Matthias and Alia.

"This place I'm thinking of—we can grow our own food there," Nina said, then explained quickly. She was careful not to say Jason's name, not to give away too much about why she'd been at Harlow School or why she'd had to leave.

Once again Percy, Matthias, and Alia exchanged glances.

"I think growing food's harder than you're making it sound," Percy said.

"But"—Matthias looked around at the prison walls—"it beats being here."

"I like trees," Alia said softly.

And with those words it was settled. Nina found herself giving the other three a genuine, full-blown smile for the very first time. She was delighted that she didn't have to dodge their gaze anymore, didn't have to try to eavesdrop on them, didn't have to worry that they knew she was supposed to betray them. There wasn't a chance anymore that she might betray them.

She was saving their lives instead.

CHAPTER SIXTEEN

The four of them decided, after much debate, to wait before they unlocked all the doors and slipped out of the prison.

"If someone got poisoned, everything will be topsy-turvy for a while," Percy said. "We should probably wait until the middle of the night."

"But the hating man—that's the guy who was interrogating me—he said no one would come to put me in the cell until eight A.M. That's, uh, ten hours away. We can get a long way away from the prison if they don't discover us missing for ten hours."

"An hour," Matthias said, as though the decision was his and his alone. "We'll wait an hour. That'll give the guards time to settle down. And"—he glanced back at the door to the jail cell—"in case someone comes to check, the three of us ought to go back in there for now."

Nina could tell from his face—and Alia's and Percy's—how much they all hated that idea. With freedom only an hour away, going back into the jail cell seemed like an unbearable punishment. Just peering into the dark beyond the door made Nina shiver. She was glad she, at least, got to stay in the hall under the glow of a lightbulb, even a weak one.

"Lock us in," Percy said quietly.

The three kids stepped over the threshold of the cell and pulled the door shut. Nina turned the key in the lock. The bolt slid into place with a permanent-sounding *thud.*

Not me, Nina thought. *I wouldn't have gone back in there. I couldn't have.* If it'd been her, she would have taken her chances, ready to risk losing all possibility of escape just to avoid sitting in the dark, damp, miserable cell for one more hour. But none of the others had murmured so much as a word of protest.

Nina spent the next hour pacing—from the door of the jail cell to the metal door that led out to the stairs, and back again. Again and again and again. It would have made sense to conserve her energy, to save her muscles and her shoe leather for the hours of walking that lay ahead. But Nina couldn't sit still, couldn't rest for a second. When she felt sure that an hour had passed, she knocked at the door of the jail cell.

"Now?" she called through the wood.

"Not yet," Matthias's muffled voice came back.

Nina paced some more. She sat down and looked through her food bag. (She kept her back toward the metal door, figuring she'd have to hide everything quickly if she heard anyone opening the door from the other side.) The biscuits were crumbled now, the apples were bruised, the oranges were starting to go soft. Was this really enough food for all four of them?

You can still leave without the others, an evil voice whispered in her head. *It's not too late to change your mind.*

No, Nina told herself firmly. She went back and knocked on the wood door again.

"Nobody's come," she said. "Nobody's going to come. It's time to go."

"Okay," one of the boys answered. She couldn't even tell which one.

She unlocked the door, and the others came out. They looked calm and unworried, as if they were off to a picnic, instead of escaping from the Population Police. Nina began trying keys in the outer door again.

"Can I?" Percy asked.

Nina hesitated. She'd been so worried about getting the others to trust her, she hadn't even thought that she might not be able to trust them. What if Percy grabbed the keys, pushed Nina back, escaped without her?

He was a nine-year-old kid. Nina handed the key ring over. Percy looked at the keyhole, sorted through the keys, then held up a dull silver one.

"Try this one next," he said.

Nina stabbed it into the hole. It fit. The lock clicked and the door gave way. The stairs lay right ahead of them, deserted and dim.

"Should one of us go up to make sure it's safe?" Nina whispered.

"Me," Alia said.

Nina waited for one of the boys to say, "Oh, no, not you." How could they send the youngest out first? But no one said anything, so Nina didn't, either. Alia tiptoed forward, as graceful and silent as the cats Nina had seen on TV. When Alia got to the top, she turned around, waved back at them, and mouthed the words, "All clear." Percy and Matthias stepped forward, and Nina followed.

"She's done that before," Nina whispered. "She's used to being the lookout."

"Shh," Matthias said over his shoulder.

By the time they reached the door to the officers' suite, Nina was convinced she was hanging out with a bunch of professional thieves. Maybe she was. What did she know about the other three kids, anyway?

I knew they were going to die if I didn't help them, Nina told herself. *That's what matters.* And anyhow, it was wonderful to have Percy, at every door, select the exact right key, without any hesitation, any noisy fumbling. It was wonderful to have Alia slipping forward, always watching, always ready to warn them. Nina felt safer with the other kids.

But at the door to the officers' suite Matthias held Nina back.

"Isn't there another way out?" he asked.

"Not that I know of," she answered. "Why?"

He pointed to gray wires running along the doorframe, so thin and nondescript Nina would never have noticed them on her own.

"Security system," Matthias muttered.

Panic welled in Nina's chest. How could they turn back now, when they were so close?

But how could they get past a security system?

CHAPTER SEVENTEEN

Nina blinked hard, trying to hold back tears.

"That's it, then," she said in a voice clotted with disappointment.

But the others weren't turning around. They didn't even look upset.

"How many more doors are there before we're out?" Matthias asked.

"Just one," Nina said. "Into the interrogation room. Then we can go out the window. I mean, we could have." She looked down, scuffing the toe of her boot against the filthy floor.

When she looked up again, Alia was scrambling up onto Matthias's shoulders. She swayed, raising her arms toward the security system wire.

"Steady," Percy said.

"What are you doing?" Nina asked.

"Cutting the wire," Alia said. She reached into the pocket of her skirt and pulled out a knife.

"Isn't that dangerous?" Nina asked. She didn't know much about security systems, but Gran and the aunties had always warned her to stay away from outlets and wires.

"Yeah," Alia said. "That's why I'm being careful."

It didn't look like she was being careful. It looked like she was sawing at the wire, making the cut as jagged and rough as possible. Alia had scraped the plastic coating off a wide section of the wire. Some of the gray coating was even floating down to the floor.

"They'll notice that right away," Nina said.

"They'll notice as soon as their monitors go black," Percy answered. "But this way, it'll look like some mice chewed on the wire, not like some prisoners were trying to escape."

"Got the key ready?" Alia asked through her clenched teeth.

"Ready," Percy said, standing as close to the door as possible. He glanced back over his shoulder at Nina. "As soon as she makes the final cut, we run. Got it?"

Nina nodded and moved over to stand behind Percy.

Alia jerked the knife one last time, letting out a stifled "Ooh!" of pain. Percy stabbed a key into the lock and turned. Alia jumped down from Matthias's shoulders and rushed through the door beside Nina. Percy was already attacking the door into the interrogation room.

"It's our lucky day," he breathed. "It's unlocked."

Nina ran through the door and shoved open the window. All four of the kids tumbled out together. The branches of the shrubs scratched Nina's arms and pulled at her dress, but she kept moving, rolling on down the hill.

The food sack bumped against her legs. Out of the corner of her eye she saw that Matthias stayed behind, pulling the window down behind him.

"Come on!" Percy hissed in Nina's ear. "Head for the trees."

Half running, half falling, Nina dashed blindly behind Percy and Alia. They were fast. In the darkness Nina was terrified that she'd lose them. She found herself navigating more by sound than by sight. As long as she could hear the other kids panting, she was okay.

The grass she was running through grew thicker, pulled more at her ankles. No, it wasn't grass—it was scrub brush on the floor of the woods. They were surrounded by trees now.

"All right," Matthias said softly, right behind her. Somehow he'd caught up. "Let's stop and watch now."

Nina wanted to keep running, but Percy put his hand on her shoulder, held her in place. The other kids crouched down, so Nina did, too, peering back at the prison.

Now that she was away from the prison, Nina could see that what the hating man had told her was true—the prison did have high barbed-wire fences and guard stations and bright lights at the back. The officers' quarters, where they'd escaped from, was just a small, one-story addition on an unprotected side. It was swathed in darkness. Nina had to squint to see it against the glare of the rest of the prison.

"They're not looking for us yet," Matthias mumbled.

"No—there! Look!" Percy breathed, pointing.

A dim light—a flashlight?—shone briefly through the window they'd climbed out of. Then the light disappeared, and reappeared in another window of the officers' quarters.

"Nobody's coming outside," Matthias muttered. "We fooled them."

Nina shivered, thinking about what might have happened if Matthias had left the window open; if Alia had cut the security system wire straight out, instead of making it look like the work of an animal's teeth.

"What would we have done if they'd come looking for us?" Nina asked.

"Hidden," Percy said matter-of-factly. "We're good at hiding."

"You're good at a lot of things," Nina said wonderingly. "I . . ." She wanted to thank them, to admit that she wouldn't have been able to escape without them. But the other three were already standing up, getting ready to move on.

"Moon's coming up over there, so that's east," Percy said. "Which direction is this safe place you were telling us about?"

Nina looked around, from the full moon's glow to the glare of the prison lights to the darkness of the woods beyond. The panic that had been threatening all night finally overwhelmed her.

"I don't know!" she wailed. "I don't know how to get there!"

CHAPTER EIGHTEEN

The other three kids didn't even look surprised. Nina felt more ashamed than ever, that they had expected her not to know, expected her to be stupid and ignorant.

"Calm down," Matthias said, none too gently. "We can think this through." He looked over at Percy expectantly.

"The place you think is safe, it's by the school you used to go to, right?" Percy asked.

Nina nodded.

"And the Population Police brought you to prison from your school, right?"

Nina nodded again.

"What time of day was it when they brought you here?"

For a minute Nina was afraid she wasn't even going to be able to answer that question. But she recovered quickly, her mind supplying a frightening jumble of images.

"Morning," she said. "They arrested me at breakfast." She could still smell the oatmeal, could still see those three lonely raisins hiding among the oats. The memory made her want to gag.

"Okay. Good," Percy said encouragingly, like he was talking to a really little kid, even younger than Alia. "Now, think carefully. When they were driving you here, what side of the car was the sun on?"

"The sun?" Nina wasn't sure she'd heard the question right. Then she wasn't sure she could answer it. She'd just been arrested by the Population Police, she'd been terrified out of her wits—who in their right mind would pay attention to the sun at a time like that? Then she remembered the splat of water on the car window beside her, the flow of drops on the glass. "The sun wasn't even out," she said triumphantly. "It was raining."

Percy and Matthias exchanged glances. Nina got an inkling that she shouldn't be feeling so triumphant.

"Why does it matter?" she asked.

"If we knew what side of the car the sun was on," Matthias explained, "we'd know which direction you were traveling. The sun is on the east side of the sky in the morning. If it was raining and the sun wasn't out, we don't know where you were coming from."

"Oh," Nina said. Though she couldn't see clearly enough, Nina had the distinct feeling that Matthias had spoken through gritted teeth.

It wasn't fair to expect Nina to know about the sun and the sky. She'd seen so little of either of them in her lifetime. What made Percy and Matthias such experts?

"Can you think hard?" Percy was asking patiently. "Was there any part of the sky that was brighter than the rest of the sky that morning?"

This was like Aunty Lystra's detective shows. The detectives were always saying things like, "I know it's a strain, ma'am, but it's important for you to remember—are you sure you heard Mr. X leave his room before midnight?" But in Aunty Lystra's shows the witnesses were always sure of themselves: "Oh, yes. I heard his door open just before the midnight train went through, just before the clock chimed." Nina hadn't been looking at the sky when the Population Police brought her to prison. She'd been looking down, at the cuffs on her wrists, the chains on her ankles. But if she'd looked out long enough to see the rain . . .

"It was still dark when we left the school," Nina said slowly. "But then, I think . . . I think there was kind of a glow in the sky, through the rain, out my window."

"Sunrise," Matthias muttered.

"The sun rises?" Nina asked. She'd never thought about how it got up into the sky. In pictures and on TV it was just there, overhead.

Percy ignored her question and asked one of his own: "Which side of the car were you on?"

"Left side. In the back," Nina said.

"So the left side's east—you were going south," Percy announced.

"If you say so," Nina said.

"Her school's probably right off Route One," Matthias said. "North of the city. Do we dare walk alongside the road?"

"If we don't, we'll be lost for sure," Percy said.

Nina noticed how they didn't even pretend to ask her opinion. At least both boys glanced quickly at Alia, long enough for her to nod her agreement.

Nina told herself she didn't care. She just hoped she was right about the direction of the sunrise.

CHAPTER NINETEEN

The four of them trudged through the woods for hours. Nina got so tired that she stopped paying attention to where she was going, what the others said, or anything else. All that mattered was forcing herself to pick up one foot after the other, putting each foot down a little farther ahead of the other. She remembered how she'd told herself the other kids might slow her down—what a joke. *She* was the slow one. *She* was the one the others turned around and waited for, impatiently.

Finally Alia danced back to Nina and took her hand and said, "You can sit down now. We're going to wait while . . . while Percy and Matthias do something."

Nina sank down to the ground and let her head flop back against a tree trunk. It felt better than any pillow.

"Do you want something to eat?" she said drowsily.

"Oh, yes!" Alia said. "Can I?"

Nina untied the food bag from around her waist and opened it toward the little girl.

"Take whatever you want," Nina said.

"I think—just something small," Alia decided. "Until

the boys come back. They'll know how to make the food stretch out."

Nina didn't even bother staying awake to see what Alia chose. The next thing she knew, Alia was gently sliding an orange slice into Nina's mouth.

"This will give you energy," Alia said.

Nina chewed and swallowed. She hadn't had oranges much. This one was sweet and juicy. And one slice wasn't nearly enough. All it did was remind Nina how ravenous she was. She pawed through the food bag and pulled out a box of cereal. She ripped off the top and began pouring it into her mouth. She'd never gobbled anything down so quickly before in her life.

"It's your food, not ours," Alia said. "But shouldn't you save some to make sure we have enough for our trip?"

In the dark Nina hadn't even realized that Alia could see what she was doing. Nina blushed and stopped chewing. She'd been eating so greedily that some of the cereal flakes had bounced off her face and fallen to the ground, ruined.

"Did Percy and Matthias say you were my boss while they were gone?" Nina grumbled.

"No," Alia said.

Nina began picking cereal out of the box, one flake at a time, and carefully placing each flake on her tongue.

"Where are they, anyway?"

"Um, they can tell you when they get back," Alia said uncertainly.

This was maddening. Nina felt like throwing the whole box of cereal at the little girl. But just then she saw a glimmer of light bobbing through the woods. Coming toward them.

"Alia, look!" Nina whispered. "It's the Population Police. They're following our trail! We've got to run. . . ." She jumped up, only barely managing not to spill the rest of the cereal.

"Nina, relax. It's Percy and Matthias," Alia answered.

"How do you know?"

"That's our signal. The way the light jumps."

Nina looked again, and it did seem like the light was bobbing in a particular pattern: twice to the right, once to the left. Then twice to the right, once to the left again.

"Where'd they get a flashlight?" Nina asked.

Alia didn't answer.

A few minutes later the light went out. A twig crackled behind Nina and she stiffened, but it was only Percy and Matthias, sneaking closer.

"Safe?" Alia asked.

"Yep," Percy said.

"Where were you? Where'd you get the flashlight?" Nina asked.

"We found it. Wasn't that lucky?" Matthias said.

Nina noticed he had answered only one of her questions. And she didn't entirely believe that answer. Flashlights were valuable, especially if they had batteries. She'd never even seen one until she went away to school.

Who would leave a flashlight just lying around out in the woods?

"Nina offered us food," Alia said.

Nina fought down her irritation. She hadn't offered *them* food—she'd shared it with Alia. And why did she get the feeling that Alia was mostly trying to change the subject? But she couldn't think of anything to do but hold out the food bag with an ungracious, "Here."

Percy and Matthias each pulled out a box of raisins.

"It's almost dawn," Percy said. "I think it's safe for us to rest for a while. We can take turns sitting sentry."

"Sentry?" Nina asked. "You mean—"

"One person watches while the others sleep," Alia said.

Nina narrowed her eyes, thinking. Alia sounded like she knew all about sitting sentry.

"I can go first," Nina said. "I got some sleep already, while you were out 'finding' things." She hoped they would notice the ironic twist she put on those words, but nobody said anything.

Within minutes, it seemed, the others were sound asleep, curled up together in a heap on the ground. Nina stared out into half darkness that seemed to be filled with mysteries. She wanted to turn on the flashlight, as if light could be company for her. But it was too dangerous—the light would only advertise their location to anyone who might be nearby. And the flashlight was too much of a mystery itself. Just thinking about it scared Nina.

Nina turned around and looked at the other three kids.

As the darkness faded, Nina watched the other kids' features emerge from the shadows. She'd spent so much time with them without light, she'd never had a chance to really study their faces. In sleep, Alia looked sweet and cute and cuddly. Even though she had a streak of dirt across her cheek, her light hair was neatly pulled back into a ponytail at the nape of her neck. Her dress was ragged and dirty, but the rips in the skirt had been mended with tiny, meticulous stitches. Nina wondered who had sewn those stitches, who had done Alia's hair. Had Percy and Matthias been sitting in the darkness of the jail cell every day carefully combing Alia's hair? Where had they learned to do that?

Maybe Alia had done it all herself. Nina remembered how confidently she'd climbed the stairs back at the prison, how confidently she'd turned back and mouthed the words, "All clear." Where had Alia learned to be a lookout?

Nina looked out into the woods again—after all, *she* was supposed to be the lookout now—but nothing stirred. Not so much as a fern frond moved in the wind. She turned her gaze back to the other kids, settling this time on Percy. Everything about Percy was sharp—his nose, the set of his mouth, the bony elbows jutting out of his oversized, rolled-up shirtsleeves. His dark hair was longish and tangled. If he was the one who served as Alia's hairstylist, he used up all his effort on her and didn't do a thing for himself.

Huddled against Percy's back, Matthias looked worried, even in his sleep. His eyes squinted together and he moaned softly, as if he was having a bad dream. He turned his head from side to side, and his brown hair flopped down over his eyes.

What did Matthias dream about? What did he think about? Who was he, anyhow? She wondered, vaguely, if he'd killed someone to get the flashlight. For a minute, she could almost imagine it. It didn't seem impossible. So now the Population Police wouldn't be looking just for escaped prisoners, but murderers as well.

Nina shivered. Any way she looked at it, she was lost in a strange woods, in danger, with three kids she didn't trust. For all she knew, they could be like Jason—ready to betray her at any second. Crazy ideas sprouted in her mind: Maybe they were planning to kill her and steal her food. Maybe they were trying to figure out a way to turn her in to the Population Police and get a reward, without getting caught themselves. Maybe Nina should be running away from them right now, as fast as she could.

Alia sighed softly in her sleep, and that sound was enough to stop Nina's panic. Nina wasn't sure what to make of Percy and Matthias—after all, the last boy she'd trusted had betrayed her. But surely sweet, lovable Alia couldn't be in on a plot to hurt Nina.

Could she?

Nina stared back into the woods again, a strange, wild place with branches jutting out at odd angles and vines hanging down like curtains. Nina couldn't have said if this woods looked like the one by her school or not. She'd never seen the other woods by daylight, only groped through it in the dark, clinging to Jason's hand. This sunlit woods was a terrifying place. The leaves on the trees seemed to hide eyes; the underbrush was probably crawling with snakes. Worse yet, Nina had no idea which way she was supposed to go to get to safety. But Percy did. Matthias did. Probably even Alia did.

Whether Nina wanted to trust the other kids or not, she had to.

She couldn't survive without them.

CHAPTER TWENTY

Nina fell asleep.

She didn't mean to, but it was too hard to fight after walking all night. She kept telling herself to keep her eyes open—just a little longer, just until someone else woke up—but even her own eyes tricked her. They slid shut while she wasn't paying attention, and the next thing she knew, she was jerking awake, panicked.

"What? Who?" she sputtered senselessly.

Birds sang overhead. The day was hot now. Even in the shade of the woods Nina could feel sweat trickling down her back. But no Population Police officer stared down at her, no vicious snake hissed at her feet, no nightmare-come-to-life stood before her.

And everyone else was still asleep.

Alia's eyelids fluttered.

"Is it my turn?" she said drowsily.

"No, no, go back to sleep," Nina managed to reply.

But Percy was stirring now, too; Matthias was stretching and yawning. He squinted up at the sky.

"It's after noon now. Were you sentry the whole time?"

he asked Nina. "Thanks for letting the rest of us sleep."

"No problem," Nina said uncomfortably. She couldn't bring herself to admit that she'd been sleeping, too. Nothing had happened, so it didn't really matter. Did it?

Percy was looking up at the sun, too. You'd think it was a clock and a map, the way they acted.

"I bet we can make it to your safe place by nightfall," he told Nina.

Nina shrugged, not wanting to ask how he knew that.

"Can we have some breakfast?" Alia asked in her sweet, little-girl voice.

"Lunch, you mean," Matthias corrected her.

Reluctantly Nina hauled out her food sack. By daylight it looked ragged and gross. But she was too hungry to care. She pulled an oatmeal bar out for herself and handed the sack on to Matthias. He selected a crumbly biscuit.

"These will go moldy if we don't eat them first," he said, and Nina heard the criticism in his voice, that Nina had picked something else.

Percy and Alia also chose biscuits. The oatmeal stuck in Nina's throat.

"We're going to need water," she mumbled. "I'm so thirsty. Can people die without water?"

It was amazing what she didn't know, what she'd never needed to know before. Being raised by Gran and the aunties—doted over, cosseted, her every need anticipated and met—wasn't exactly good training for surviving in the woods. Harlow School hadn't taught her anything useful, either.

"There's a river up ahead," Percy said.

This time Nina did ask, "How do you know?"

"I can hear it," he answered.

And then Nina heard it, too, a distant hum, barely audible over the chirping of birds and the sound of the wind in the trees. Was that how water sounded?

"Let's go, then," Nina said. She was afraid suddenly that her throat might close over, that she might die of thirst right then and there.

"We have to clean up first," Matthias said.

Nina had her mouth open to ask what he meant—there was dirt everywhere, how did he expect to clean up a woods? But he and Percy and Alia had already gone to work, picking up crumbs, ruffling up the grass they'd slept on and flattened, erasing all signs of their presence.

"How did you know to do that?" Nina asked.

Percy shrugged. "We're not stupid," he answered. Nina heard the words he didn't say: "Not like you."

Nina turned away so no one could see how hurt she was. The others began walking toward the sound of the river, and she followed at a distance, her throat aching.

The hum of the water got louder the closer they got. It was like the buzz of traffic Nina had been able to hear in the summer, when they kept the windows open, at the apartment she'd shared with Gran and the aunties. The sound made Nina strangely homesick. *If Gran could see me now,* she thought. *Filthy, ragged, disgusting. Desperate.* Gran used to scrub Nina's whole face if she had so much as a speck of jam by her mouth. No matter how much heating oil cost, Gran insisted on heating Nina's bathwater until Nina felt parboiled every time she bathed. "Kills germs," Gran always said.

The memories stuck in Nina's mind as she fell to her knees before the river and, like the others, scooped water into her hands to drink and drink and drink. When she'd slaked her thirst, she announced to the others, "I'm taking a bath here, too."

They stared at her.

"We're filthy," Nina said. "I haven't had a bath since they arrested me. You guys should wash up, too."

"Do you know how to swim?" Percy asked.

"No," Nina admitted. She stared out across the wide river. Was it deep, too? "I'll stay close to the edge."

She untied the food bag from around her waist and hung it on a branch high over the others' heads. She hoped they wouldn't notice that she didn't trust them. Then she took off her boots and stockings and, still in her dress, eased into the water.

Mud squished between her toes, and she hesitated. Could she get clean, or would the muddy water only make her dirtier? But the water felt cool and wonderful against her skin. She took another step forward, bent down, and scooped water onto her arms, rubbing off the prison grime. She splashed water up against her face and into her hair.

She unbraided her hair and dipped her whole head in. She lifted her feet from the river bottom, and the current carried her downstream a little. She put her feet down again.

"Come on in," she urged the others. "It's great!"

She saw Alia glance questioningly back at Matthias. Matthias shrugged. Alia began taking off her heavy boots.

"Look! I'm swimming!" Nina shouted, moving her arms the way she'd seen swimmers do on TV. She lowered her head and felt her hair stream out behind her, floating on the water. She felt happier than she'd felt since she'd been arrested, since she'd found out that Jason had betrayed her, since the hating man had asked her to betray Percy, Matthias, and Alia. Water flowed past her, and the current seemed almost strong enough to carry away all her hurt and anger and suspicions. Behind her, she could hear Alia giggling.

"I'm a fish!" Nina said, and ducked underwater. Her dress weighed her down and the skirt tangled in her legs, but it didn't matter. She floated with the water bugs, then surfaced to let the sun warm her skin again.

"Don't go out too far," Percy warned from the side.

"I'm fine!" Nina yelled back. "It's not over my head. The bottom's right . . . right . . ." She reached her foot down—and down—and down. No friendly mud touched her toes. The next thing she knew, her head slipped underwater.

She flailed her arms and thrust her head up long enough to gulp in some air. Her clothes felt even heavier now, pulling her down, down, down. The current pushed at her, faster and faster, carrying her away from Percy, Matthias, and Alia. Frantically Nina shoved at the water, trying to fight her way back to the shore.

And then she put her foot down again, and miraculously, there was solid ground there again.

"I'm okay!" Nina called back to the others. "Don't worry!"

She stood still, savoring the feel of mud squishing through her toes—lifesaving mud. Everything had happened so fast, her mind hadn't had time fully to grasp what might have happened, but she could have drowned, fooling around. How silly it would have been, to survive Jason's betrayal, to survive the Population Police's jail, only to die taking a bath.

She looked around, appreciating every safe, wonderful breath she drew into her lungs, every chirp of birdsong she heard in the trees around her. And then her eyes began to register the view in slow motion. It wasn't just trees and river and sky around her. The river had carried her around a bend. Right in front of her was a bridge, a huge, ugly Government-made concrete bridge. And on the bridge, leaning over the edge, were two men in uniform. Two men in uniform, leaning over, opening their mouths, yelling.

Nina seemed to hear their words at a slower than normal speed, too.

"You there! In the river! That's not allowed! Come out and show us your I.D.!"

CHAPTER TWENTY-ONE

If only Nina could swim. She wanted to dive back into the water, swim for miles without surfacing once. Escape.

Failing that, she needed to jump out of the water, run through the woods, hope she could disappear into the trees. But the Population Police would only start a manhunt here, comb through the whole area. She didn't have a chance.

All those images—swimming, running, being caught—flashed through Nina's mind in an instant. She even saw Percy and Matthias and Alia being caught with her. It would be all Nina's fault. She had betrayed them after all.

Nina froze in agony. Her mind wouldn't supply a single response she could give to the uniformed men, a single method of buying even a second more to think.

Then she heard Alia's voice behind her.

"Just a minute," the little girl said. "My sister and I left our I.D.'s with our shoes on the shore."

Okay, Nina thought, a part of her mind surprisingly lucid despite her terror. *That gives me an extra minute or two. I should have thought of that. But won't it make the policemen angrier when they discover she's lying?*

"Get your I.D.'s, then," one of the men on the bridge growled.

Nina looked back over her shoulder. Alia disappeared around the bend.

It's not fair, Nina thought. *Now Alia and the boys are going to be safe, and I'm not.* She could just imagine Alia and Percy and Matthias running now, getting as far away from the river as possible. Sure, Alia had given Nina a little extra time—but what good was that? How long before the Population Policemen on the bridge realized Alia wasn't coming back? What would they do to Nina then?

But there was Alia, wading back toward Nina, carrying two plastic cards in her hand. Nina gaped, strained her neck to see what Alia was holding. Alia drew even with Nina, slipped her fingers into Nina's hand, and pulled her along.

"Don't look so surprised," Alia hissed out of the side of her mouth. "Let me do all the talking."

That wouldn't be hard. Nina was so stunned, she didn't think she even had a voice anymore. For she'd glimpsed the cards in Alia's hand, and they looked like ordinary I.D.'s. One was stamped, SUSAN BROWN. The other said, JANICE BROWN.

And they contained Alia's and Nina's pictures.

No—Nina looked again—it wasn't really their pictures. But the resemblance was so close, Nina was sure the policemen would be fooled. As long as she and Alia didn't make any mistakes.

Alia held the I.D.'s as carelessly as if they were just some pretty leaves she'd picked up off the ground.

They reached the shore, and still Alia marched forward, Nina trailing by a few steps. The brush growing at the water's edge poked her ankles and pricked her feet. She stepped gingerly, half stumbling. Alia's strong grip held her up.

"It's illegal to swim in that river," one of the men said sternly. "That's Government property. We could arrest you for trespassing."

Alia held out the I.D.'s for his inspection. He took them, glanced at them quickly, then handed them to the other man.

"Well?" the first man said. "Aren't you scared of being arrested?"

"Oh, please don't arrest us," Alia said, her little-girl voice sounding even more sweet and childish than ever. "We're going to visit our grandmother, and we slipped in the mud. We couldn't let her see us like that. We thought we could just wash off quickly—we didn't know we were breaking any laws. We're sorry."

"Where does your grandmother live?"

"Terrazzine," Alia said confidently. Nina had never heard of the place.

"Doesn't your sister talk?" the second man said, handing the I.D. cards back to Alia. Alia stuffed them in her pocket.

"No, sir," Alia said, just as Nina was opening her mouth to answer. Nina closed her mouth and hoped nobody had noticed. "My sister's mute, sir. And not quite right in the head, if you know what I mean. I have to take care of her, my mother says."

"Well, you're a brave little thing," the first man said. "We'll let you off, this time. But you be careful, and stay on the road from now on, you hear? We're not far from the Population Police prison, you know. I've been saying for years, if any of those prisoners escaped—"

"I know, sir," Alia said, seeming to quell a shiver of fear. "My mother has told us about the prison."

The policemen turned in one direction, and Alia and Nina went the other way. Nina noticed for the first time that Alia had her boots and Nina's looped around her neck, tied together by the shoelaces.

"Here. Let's put our shoes back on, Janice dear," Alia said, a little too loudly.

Dumbly Nina stuck out first one foot and then the other, and let Alia cram her stockings and boots on. She heard a car roaring away behind her. The policemen were gone.

Nina sagged against a tree in relief.

"What . . . how did you—"

"Shh," Alia said. "Sometimes they come back and check out your story. It's not safe for you to talk yet. But keep walking."

She tugged on Nina's hand, and Nina obediently kept

pace beside the younger girl. They were walking down the middle of the road now, in plain sight, for anyone to see.

"Can't you explain as we walk?" Nina grumbled, trying not to move her lips.

"Nope," Alia said.

The sun beat down from overhead. The woods fell away alongside the road, and they walked past scattered houses and scraggly fields. This was countryside Nina had seen twice before—coming to school and then leaving it—but she'd been inside a car and numb with fear both times. She was beyond numbness now. Her mind kept replaying her moments of terror—the water pulling her under, the policeman yelling, "Come out and show us your I.D.!" And Alia coming to her rescue.

"When it's safe to talk," Nina said quietly, "when we meet up with Percy and Matthias again, the three of you are going to tell me everything. And . . . and I'm going to tell you everything, too."

Alia flashed her a look that Nina couldn't read. It might have meant, "Quit talking." It might have meant, "You're crazy if you think we're telling you anything."

But it also might have meant, "All right. It's time to share."

CHAPTER TWENTY-TWO

Alia and Nina had reached the driveway to Harlow School for Girls before Alia deemed it safe to talk.

"Is that your school over there?" Alia asked quietly when they rounded a bend in the road.

Nina stared out at the expanse of grass and the imposing three-story brick building. The school had no windows—that had seemed so natural from the inside, when Nina wasn't used to seeing out windows anyhow. But from the outside the lack of windows looked odd, as if the building were supposed to be a monument or a memorial, not any place that people could live.

"That's it," Nina said. "And the woods are behind the school."

She pointed. Alia nodded and detoured around the school, skulking behind bushes and shrubs.

"What about Percy and Matthias? And . . . and our food?" Nina didn't want to seem more concerned about her food sack than the two boys. But it was hard not to be, what with her stomach growling.

"They'll find us," Alia said confidently.

A few minutes later they entered the coolness of the woods. Alia sat down on a stump, and Nina sank onto the ground beside her. She took off her boots and rubbed her sore feet.

"How far do you think we walked?" Nina asked.

"Couple of miles," Alia said.

"How did you know how to get here?"

"There aren't that many roads in use anymore," Alia said. "Percy thought this would be the right way." She looked around the woods and said cheerfully, "This is a nice place."

"I guess," Nina said doubtfully. She watched a spider climb into her boot. Were spiders poisonous? Would she survive the Population Police prison, a near drowning, and the long escape only to die of a spider bite?

Alia reached over and shook the spider out of Nina's boot. The spider scampered away.

"Thanks," Nina muttered. She wondered if she'd ever get used to being outdoors. It didn't seem natural not to have four walls around her, a ceiling above her head, and a solid floor beneath her feet. Jason had always teased the kids who were scared of the woods. *No, no,* she chided herself, *don't think about Jason ever again.* Still. The woods were unpleasant enough now, in the warm sunshine. What would they be like when it was raining, or when winter came?

Alia obviously didn't care. She began whistling, sounding as carefree as a bird. Her whistle evidently tricked birds, too, because one called back to her, "Tweet-tweet," in answer to her "Tweet-tweet-tweet."

And then Nina realized it wasn't another bird, but Percy and Matthias. They stepped up quietly behind her.

"Safe?" Alia asked.

"Safe," Matthias answered.

The boys sat down beside Nina. As if they'd all agreed ahead of time, Percy opened the food bag and handed out what seemed to be a feast: a box of cereal, a box of raisins, and an apple for everyone. Nina didn't object. Matthias raised his apple like he was making a toast: "To our new home," he said.

"To roughing it," Percy said.

"To Nina's idea," Alia said.

Nina looked from face to face, then raised her own apple and said, "To my new friends getting us here safely."

Eating required full concentration. Chewing and swallowing was such a joy that no one spoke until they were down to the cores of their apples, picking out the last bits of flesh from among the seeds. Then Nina said what she'd worked out during her long, silent walk with Alia.

"The three of you are used to roughing it," she said. "I don't know where you lived before you were arrested, but it was outdoors. And I don't know how, but you made fake I.D.'s for third children. That's what Percy and Matthias went to get last night when we were running away. When you brought back the flashlight."

Nina waited while the other three exchanged glances. Alia nodded, ever so slightly at the other two.

"Yes," Percy said softly. "You're right."

"Why didn't you tell me we had I.D.'s?" Nina asked. "We could have gone somewhere else if we didn't have to hide. Somewhere with walls and a roof and a floor."

"Where?" Matthias asked. "I.D.'s aren't food. They aren't rent money. They aren't adults to answer nosy questions from the Government. I.D. cards are just pieces of plastic."

Nina shrugged. Before she was arrested, she'd never lacked for food or shelter or adult care. All she'd ever missed was a legal identity. She tried a different tack.

"I could have given everything away when the Population Police saw me," she said. "Since I didn't know you'd made an I.D. card for me, I was about to scream and run. Then they would have known—"

"You thought those guys were Population Policemen?" Percy asked incredulously. "Population Police would have known to look for runaways. Those guys were just local cops. Minor league. They probably hate the Population Police as much as we do."

Nina tried to absorb this news. "But—"

"Look, the Population Police wouldn't tell anyone else that someone had escaped from their prison. It'd be like . . . like a blow to their pride. They like everyone to think that they're invincible, impossible to beat. So it's just Population Policemen looking for us. And if they ask the local cops, the local cops won't tell them about seeing two girls on the northbound road out of the city. That's why we're safe," Matthias said.

Nina wondered how he could sound so sure.

"We lived on the streets before," Alia said softly. "In the city. We know how things work."

Nina tried to imagine it. No wonder the other three had always looked so grubby. But how had they managed it? How had they gotten food? How had they avoided being arrested years ago?

"Who took care of you?" Nina asked.

"God took care of us," Alia said. "We prayed to him and he took care of us. Just like we prayed in prison and he sent us you to get us out."

Nina had heard of God before. Gran, for one, had prayed back home, even though Aunty Lystra made fun of her for it.

"That's one thing the Government's right about," Aunty Lystra had said. "If there were a God out there who really cared about us, do you think we'd be living like this?" "This" seemed to encompass everything from the leaky roof to the weevils in the flour to the long line at the store for cabbage.

"You believe what you want to believe, and I'll believe what I want to believe," Gran always answered. "I, for one, see a few miracles around here."

Nina had liked the way Gran's eyes rested on her when she said that. Even when Nina was too tiny to understand the word "miracle," she'd liked it, liked the way Gran talked about God.

But she didn't understand how God could take care of three little kids alone on the streets.

"I'm thirsty," Percy announced, with a warning glance toward Alia. "Let's go find some water and explore a little."

The other three scrambled up. Nina pulled her boots back on and followed, thinking hard.

They hadn't told her everything, after all. And so she hadn't said a word about her past, either.

CHAPTER TWENTY-THREE

The days that followed the kids' arrival in the woods were strangely like a holiday. The sun shone down on them—just warm enough, not too hot—and they had fun hiking around, exploring. They slept under the stars each balmy night. Nina did not exactly forget Jason's betrayal and the nightmare of prison, but all the horrors she'd experienced seemed far in the past. She worried less and less about being caught again. When she opened her eyes each morning to see gently waving branches and a mosaic of maple leaves against the sky, it didn't seem possible that she could be imprisoned in a dark underground room ever again.

For their part, Percy, Matthias, and Alia seemed perfectly happy to treat their time in the woods as one long vacation. They didn't talk about prison; they didn't talk about their lives before prison. They climbed trees; they skipped rocks in the stream; they drew pictures in the dirt with twigs.

Then one morning Nina reached her hand into the food bag for breakfast and closed her fingers on—nothing. She reached farther down, her stomach suddenly queasy with hunger. She brought up a small, battered box of cereal and an empty peanut shell. She laid those on her knees and reached in again.

Nothing. Truly nothing. Not even a moldy biscuit crumb remained in the sack.

"We don't have any more food!" Nina gasped.

The others paused in the midst of their own meals. Percy held a half-eaten oatmeal bar up to his mouth; Alia froze with an apple against her lips. Matthias kept chewing his cereal.

"What?" he said, his mouth full.

"We're out of food!" Nina repeated. "What you're eating now—that's all we have!"

"So is your garden ready?" Percy asked casually. "You said you could grow a garden here."

Nina gaped at him.

"I didn't . . . I meant . . ." What had she promised, in desperation, back in prison when they were planning their escape? Were the others really counting on her to provide all their food? Why hadn't they mentioned it before now? "I—Alia, give me the seeds from that apple."

Obediently Alia dug her fingernails into the middle of the apple and handed Nina three grimy brown seeds. Nina scratched in the dirt by her feet and dug three holes, side by side. She placed a seed in each hole. Then she patted dirt back over the seeds until they were hidden from sight.

"There," she said. "At least we'll have more apples."

"How long does it take?" Percy asked.

Nina stared down at the dirt, hoping something might happen right away. She suspected it took longer than a few minutes for an apple tree to grow. Probably a lot longer. And for an apple tree actually to produce apples . . .

"I don't know," she said miserably. She had a feeling it might take days, weeks, months. Years. "I don't know anything about growing food," she confessed. "I just thought we could . . . figure something out once we got here. This *is* better than being in prison, isn't it?"

"They fed us in prison," Alia said in a small voice.

"And they were going to kill us," Nina countered harshly.

Alia looked down at the ground. Percy and Matthias looked at each other. Nina couldn't stand to see them exchanging glances once again.

"Look, I'm just a kid," she pleaded. "I don't know anything about anything. My gran and the aunties—they always took care of me. Then when I got to school—well, it wasn't like they really wanted us to think for ourselves there. There was always food, three times a day. We didn't have to know where it came from."

The other three didn't say anything for a moment. In the silence, Nina could hear the wind shifting direction in the trees.

"You never told us about your gran and the . . . the aunties?" Alia finally said. "You didn't tell us about your school."

"I didn't know if I could trust you," Nina admitted. "I'm a third child. An illegal."

"We thought so," Percy said.

Silence again. Then Matthias added softly, "So are we."

Nina held her breath. The last time she'd confessed to being an illegal child, and heard someone else confess the same to her, it had led to Population Police arresting her at breakfast. She stared hard at the trees around her, as though any one of them might be hiding a Population Police officer, just waiting for the right moment to grab her. But nothing happened. No one moved.

"It's funny, isn't it," Nina said. "The reason they made third children illegal was because of food. There wasn't enough after the drought and the famines. But someone always found food for me when I was illegal. Now I've gone through two different fake I.D.'s, and I've run out of food. I'm legal now—I've got a card to prove that I'm legal—and I'm going to starve to death. We're all going to starve."

She knew now why the last few days had seemed like such a vacation. It *had* been a vacation—from reality. None of them had wanted to face the truth: It wasn't enough to escape from the Population Police. It wasn't enough to have fake I.D.'s. They were still doomed. It was easier to swing in the trees and skip rocks than to think about the fact that they had nothing to keep them alive once the food sack was empty.

"Nobody's going to starve," Percy said. "We'll figure out something. Don't you know any way to find out how to grow a garden?"

Nina started to say no, but then she remembered how she'd thought of a garden in the first place.

"There's a kid," she said. "At the boys' school. Lee Grant. He was the one who knew about gardens. If we could find him . . ."

Nina explained how she and her friends had met with the group from the boys' school. Somehow the whole story came tumbling out this time—how she and Bonner and Sally had thought they were so big, meeting guys in the woods. How she'd fallen in love with Jason. How he'd betrayed her.

The other three were silent for a long time after she finished.

"So can you trust this Lee Grant or not?" Percy asked. "Was he working with Jason?"

"I don't know," Nina said, miserable again. "He seemed okay. But . . ." She didn't finish the sentence: *Jason seemed okay, too. I thought he was a lot better than okay. How can I trust my own judgment ever again?*

"One of us will have to sneak into the school and find this Lee, and see if we can trust him," Matthias said.

"Maybe he could even give us some food from his school," Nina said. "Maybe they feed the boys better than they feed the girls."

She felt more cheerful now. Everything could work out. She waited for Percy or Matthias to volunteer to be the one to sneak into the boys' school. Matthias was closer to Lee Grant's age—if Matthias pretended to be a new student, he'd be more likely to get placed in the same classes as Lee. But Nina thought Percy was smarter—he would know what to do, how to trick Lee into telling him everything.

But neither Percy nor Matthias spoke up. Surprised, Nina looked from one boy to the other—and discovered they were both staring at her.

"Well?" she said. "Which one of you is going to do it?"

Percy waited a while longer, then shook his head in disgust, as if he couldn't believe Nina hadn't figured everything out.

"You're the only one who knows what this Lee Grant looks like. You're the only one he knows, the only one he'd be likely to trust. It's got to be you," he said.

"But I'm a girl!" Nina said. "It's a *boys'* school!"

"You can tuck your hair up in my cap," Percy said. "You can wear Matthias's clothes. You can pretend."

Nina gawked at him. She imagined herself in Matthias's ragged shirt and patched jeans, standing amidst the Hendricks boys in their fancy clothes. She'd be noticed in an instant, thrown out in a flash.

"You don't understand," she said. "I'm not like all of you. I've never had to . . . to live by my wits. If anyone stops me, I won't know what to say. That's why . . ." At the last minute, she managed to stop herself from spilling everything. *That's why I didn't know what to do when the hating man asked me to betray you. That's why I almost did betray you.* Instead she finished lamely, "That's why someone else should go instead of me. You can't trust me."

"We trust you," Alia said softly.

How could Nina disagree with that?

CHAPTER TWENTY-FOUR

It was dusk. The way the shadows slanted through the trees reminded Nina of a dozen other dusks she'd spent in the woods, when she and her friends had sneaked out to meet Jason and his buddies. Once again she was crouched behind a tree, watching and waiting. Once again she was listening for the snap of a twig, the approach of danger. Once again her heart was pounding in her chest, her every nerve ending was alert with the thrill of the risk she was about to take.

But this time she was preparing to sneak out of the woods, not into it. She pulled Matthias's cap a little lower over her eyes and peeked around the tree. She had picked dusk as the safest time for her mission. She was hoping that the boys' school, like the girls' school, had dull indoctrination sessions in the evening, which students slept through or sneaked out of. Surely she could spy on the indoctrination session, locate Lee Grant, and pull him aside as everyone was leaving. She hoped. She'd been making plans all day long.

What she hadn't counted on was how much the shadows spooked her. Not just the shadows in the trees, but the shadows that stretched across the long, long lawn between the woods and Hendricks School for Boys. If she was going to find Lee Grant, she'd have to run across those shadows, out in the open, out where someone might see.

It had been one thing to walk across the Harlow School lawn to the woods with Sally and Bonner on either side of her, giggling nervously all the way. She knew now that they had not actually expected to face real danger—only some pale imitation of it, nothing that couldn't be waved away with an I.D. card.

Nina knew she had been frightened, too, walking out in the open with Alia after they were questioned by the two policemen on the bridge. But Alia had rescued her so magically from the policemen that Nina knew she had a false sense of confidence—no matter what happened, Alia or Percy or Matthias could save her.

But the other three weren't going into Hendricks School with her now. She was completely alone.

Now I know why Gran believed in God, Nina thought. *God? Can you help me, too?*

Nina inched forward, to the edge of the woods, then threw herself into a desperate run across the lawn.

She reached the side of the building more quickly than she'd expected. She realized she'd kept her eyes squeezed shut for most of her run. She was lucky she hadn't smashed into the building. She turned around and looked back and couldn't believe she'd come all that distance, through all those shadows. She took a deep breath and clutched her fingers on to one of the bricks in the wall of the school, as if that could hold her steady.

"A door," she whispered to herself. "I need to find a door."

Sliding the palms of her hands along the wall, she moved forward, looking ahead. By the time she reached the corner, her fingertips felt ragged from the rough bricks. She didn't seem to be thinking very well. Had she missed noticing a door? Or was there one entire side of the school without any entrance at all?

Rather than turning around, she turned the corner. And there was solid metal, with a metal knob sticking out. A door and a doorknob. Just what she'd been looking for.

Without giving herself time to lose her nerve, she grabbed the knob, turned, and pulled.

A dark hallway gaped before her. She stepped into the school. The door slid shut behind her.

If Nina's heart had been pounding before, it was beating away at triple time now. Every nerve ending in her body seemed to be screaming, "Alert! Alert! Danger! Danger! Turn around and go back to safety!"

Nina was surprised her brain could still override the warning, could still make her feet slide forward. She stumbled but didn't fall, and kept moving.

The dark hall ended in a T with another dark hall. Nina turned right at first, hesitated, then turned around. Over the pounding in her ears she could hear shrieks and screams coming from the opposite direction. Somewhere down that hall boys were laughing and yelling at the top of their lungs.

It didn't sound at all like the indoctrination lectures Nina was familiar with—some dry, dusty old teacher droning on uselessly at the front of the room. This sounded like . . . like fun.

Nina crept back toward the noise, picking up speed when she realized there was no way anyone could hear her footsteps over all that commotion. Finally she reached a lit doorway that was obviously the source of all the noise. She peeked cautiously around the corner, sticking her head out just far enough to see past the doorframe.

It was a huge room, like the dining area back at Harlow School for Girls. Nina saw tables and chairs stacked against the wall—this probably was the dining room for the boys' school, but it'd been converted tonight, with boys running around chasing dozens of rubber balls across the floor.

"Kick it here!"

"No, no, I'm open!"

"Throw me the ball!"

Nina closed her eyes and slipped back out of sight around the corner of the doorframe. The boys' game had thrown her back into a memory from years before:

It was summertime. The apartment was stifling, so Aunty Lystra yanked up the windows behind the blinds, letting in little, useless whispers of breeze. But the open windows also made the noise from the street below distinct for the first time in Nina's memory. She heard little-kid voices chanting, "One potato, two potato, three potato, four . . ." She heard the thud of something—a rope?—and jumping feet hitting pavement, and voices singing, "Mama called the doctor and the doctor said . . ." Nina stood in the middle of her hot little apartment, and an expression of wonder broke over her face. "There . . . there are other kids out there," she stammered in amazement. "And they're playing. They're being loud, and it's okay. Nobody's yelling at them. Can I . . ." But the question died in her throat, because she saw the answer in Gran's eyes, in the eyes of every single one of her aunties. Other kids could play outside together and be loud. Nina couldn't. Nina would never be allowed to be like other kids.

Nina slid weakly to the floor.

How was it that the boys at Hendricks School were allowed to have fun? Nina remembered how the Harlow girls had sat like little mice through all their classes, squeaking down the hall in terror, ready to dart back into hiding at the slightest threat. It had taken Nina days to get up the nerve to whisper to Sally and Bonner in the dark of their room at night. She couldn't imagine *yelling* with them, throwing her voice across a crowded, brightly lit room.

But that was what the boys were doing.

Nina turned her head and looked again. This time she held back her sense of astonishment enough to peer at faces. Was Lee Grant in that group of wild, screaming boys?

Nina's eyes skipped from boy to boy—too small, too tall, too dark, too fair. . . . Was she even capable of remembering what Lee looked like?

Then someone yelled, "Good, good, just pick it up faster," and she recognized the voice. Maybe. She snapped her gaze over to the boy who had yelled. He was standing off to the side, swinging his arms and directing the other boys. He looked taller than Nina remembered Lee being, but maybe he had grown in the past few months. Something else was different about him, too—she couldn't quite tell what it was, but the difference was great enough that she hesitated, wondering if she'd made a mistake. Maybe this boy looked more relaxed than the Lee she remembered, maybe he grinned more confidently.

She didn't remember ever seeing Lee grin before. She couldn't imagine the Lee she'd known cheering so proudly, "That's it! That's it! You scored!"

Or slapping another boy's back so triumphantly.

Nina drew back from the door, shaken. She sat still for a long while, letting the noise from the boys' games spill over her.

She couldn't do it.

She couldn't go up to this strange boy to ask for help. He wasn't the boy she remembered—even if he was Lee Grant, she hadn't known him well enough, or he'd changed too much for her to trust him. This boy positively swaggered—he seemed as overconfident as the hating man.

Or Jason.

Nina moved farther from the door, creeping backward down the hall. She reached the other hall she'd come down and practically crawled to the door to the outside. She raised her body only high enough to turn the knob, and dropped out to the ground.

The last light of dusk was slipping away now. The woods were one huge shadow off to the left. Nina couldn't bear the thought of facing Percy, Matthias, and Alia now. Blindly she inched straight out from the school, toward another clump of shadowy plants. Maybe she could hide there, tell the others about her cowardice in the morning.

Nina reached the edge of the shadows. Something squished beneath her feet, and she wrinkled her nose in disgust. Then she sniffed.

Tomato. Suddenly the air around her smelled like tomato.

Nina reached down, groping in the dark. She felt prickly stems, delicate flowers, pointy leaves. And then she felt small, round balls. She jerked on one of the balls, pulling it off the plant. She brought the round ball up to her mouth, bit into it cautiously.

The taste of fresh tomato exploded in her mouth. Nina dropped the tomato in amazement. She took off running for the woods, forgetting all caution in her delight.

"Alia! Percy! Matthias!" she yelled. "I found a garden! We're saved!"

CHAPTER TWENTY-FIVE

They came back with the flashlight, all four of them. None of them was cautious. They shone the light from plant to plant—"Look at all the tomatoes!" "And cabbages—" "Are those green beans?" Matthias made a wondrous discovery when he tripped over a root and accidentally upended a leafy plant. A huge potato hung from the bottom of it, pulled from its hiding place in the dirt. After that, Nina pulled up other plants and found more potatoes. They gobbled them raw and didn't care. They also found underground carrots, which they ate without even cleaning.

When they'd feasted until they were full, Percy shone the light around at the toppled plants, the discarded stems, the footprints in the dirt.

"Someone's going to know," he said.

Nina raked her fingers through the soil, erasing a footprint.

"We'll cover our tracks," she said. "Like we did in the woods."

They went back and forth, carrying all the uprooted

plants out to the woods to hide. They buried the smashed tomatoes they'd carelessly knocked to the ground; they picked up every stray leaf and discarded stem.

"There," Percy said, letting one last clod of dirt filter through his fingers, covering one last trampled plant. "Is this how it looked before?"

Nina shone the flashlight back and forth. The globes of red and green looked eerie on the tomato vines. The leaves of the remaining potato plants cast shadows over the holes they'd covered so carefully.

"I don't know," she said doubtfully. It was hard to remember what the garden had looked like in the beginning; she'd been so hungry and so overjoyed at the prospect of eating. "I think next time we'll have to be more careful."

She traipsed back to the woods with the other three kids. All of them were subdued suddenly, worn out after their burst of excitement.

After that, one of them went to the garden every night and picked a day's worth of food. They tried to pick no more than one tomato from each plant and dig up no more than one potato from each row. They stayed away from the cabbages because picking a huge cabbage head would leave a gaping hole that anyone might notice. But there was still plenty of food to eat. Nina just wished some of the plants grew bread or fruit—she was getting sick of vegetables.

"If we could even cook the potatoes—," she complained one evening over raw green beans.

"Someone would see the fire," Matthias said. "They'd find us."

Percy shrugged. "At least we have food."

Nina sighed. She wished one of the others would gripe even once—about the discomfort of sleeping on roots and itchy leaves, about the rain that had fallen on them half of one night, about the muddy taste of the water they drank from the stream. But the way they acted, you'd think the woods was a palace, you'd think the raw vegetables were gourmet food. She wondered yet again about their lives before the Population Police had captured them.

"What did you eat in the city, when you were living on the streets?" she asked.

"Same kind of food as everyone else," Percy said, brushing dirt from a carrot.

"Sometimes we'd find doughnuts in the garbage outside a bakery," Alia said dreamily, as if that were one of her dearest memories.

Nina shuddered. "Didn't you make any money from selling fake I.D.'s?" she asked. "How did you manage to do that, anyway?"

"Let's just say it was a nonprofit operation," Matthias said. "Anybody mind if I have the last potato?"

Nina could tell when she'd had a door slammed in her face. Matthias had as good as said, "Don't ask any more questions." She did, anyway.

"Do you think you could start doing that again?" she asked. "And I could help you. Why didn't you think you could go back to the city and live on the streets again? I could come with you—we could work together. . . . Maybe we could even find doughnuts again." She grinned a little at Alia. Suddenly it all seemed possible—even eating doughnuts out of the garbage. The woods and the raw vegetables were only temporary. They had to make some plans beyond the next day. When the garden died . . . when winter came . . . they had to be ready.

"We were arrested when we lived in the city, remember?" Percy said harshly. "Someone betrayed us. We don't know who. So—we can't go back. We wouldn't know who to trust."

Nina blinked back tears she didn't want the others to see. She stood up.

"I'll go to the garden tonight," she mumbled. "It's my turn."

Listlessly she threaded her way between trees, stepped out onto the lawn that led to the garden. She'd forgotten the flashlight, but it didn't matter. It was still early for a trip to the garden. The shadow from the boys' school was only beginning to stretch across the lawn. The red tomatoes gleamed in the last glow of twilight.

"Tomatoes, potatoes, beans, and carrots," Nina muttered to herself. By comparison, even doughnuts plucked from a trash Dumpster sounded good. She reached the edge of the garden and picked her first vegetable: a cucumber, just for variety's sake.

Knowing that someone had betrayed the other three

kids made her feel worse than ever. Even if their story came out only in bits and pieces, she felt more like she understood them now. No wonder they hadn't wanted to trust her in the beginning, when the hating man first put her in the prison cell with them. Maybe she should tell them about the rest of her story, after Jason betrayed her. Maybe she should tell them about the hating man wanting her to betray them. Maybe then . . .

Nina didn't know what would happen if she told the others everything. Maybe it would just give them something to betray her with.

The world seemed to contain entirely too many betrayals.

Nina pulled an ear of corn from one of the stalks at the edge of the garden. She pulled back the husks, wondering if the cob inside actually contained something worth eating. None of the corn so far had been edible, but Nina still had hope. She brought the tiny nubs of grain up to her mouth, bit, and chewed thoughtfully. Not bad. She looked toward the next row of cornstalks, hoping for bigger ears.

Then she froze.

There in the cornstalks, his face distorted with anger, a boy stood glowering at her.

"You!" he hissed. "You're the one who's been stealing from my garden!"

"No, wait, I can explain—"

But the boy rushed forward, grabbed her by her wrists. Another boy joined him from behind and clutched Nina's right arm. Nina looked from one to the other. She recognized them both now.

"Lee! Trey!" she screamed. "Don't you remember me? I'm Nina. I used to meet you in the woods—"

"Yeah. And then you helped Jason try to betray us," Lee snarled back.

"I didn't! I didn't!" Nina screamed.

But it was no use. They were dragging her away.

CHAPTER TWENTY-SIX

Nina tried to dig her heels in, to hold back. She tried to yank her arms out of the boys' grasp. She remembered them both as skinny, wimpy kids—like little rabbits beside Jason's brawn. But somehow they'd developed muscles. Even squirming was useless.

Lee and Trey half pulled, half carried Nina past the school and down a driveway. Then they turned down a path. A stone cottage loomed ahead of them. Nina made one last attempt to jerk away from the boys, but they only tightened their grip.

"Where are you taking me?" Nina demanded.

"To Mr. Hendricks," Lee said abruptly.

Nina wondered who Mr. Hendricks was. It had never occurred to her that Hendricks School might have been named after a real person. Was there a Mr. Harlow, too? A Mrs. Harlow?

Nina didn't know how she could wonder such things at a time like this. They were in front of the cottage now, and Lee was pounding on the door.

"Mr. Hendricks! Mr. Hendricks! We found the thief!"

The door opened. Nina, looking straight ahead, didn't see anyone there. Then she looked down, like the boys were doing.

A man in a wheelchair sat before them.

"Indeed," he said.

Lee jerked on Nina's arm, drew her into the house.

"And what do you have to say for yourself, young lady?" Mr. Hendricks asked when all three kids stood before him in the foyer.

Nina opened her mouth, but nothing came out.

"Surely you have something to say, some defense to give," Mr. Hendricks said.

"I don't know what to tell you," Nina blurted. "I don't know whose side you're on."

Mr. Hendricks chuckled.

"Then I guess you'll have to tell me the truth," he said.

Everyone waited. Nina kept her teeth clenched firmly together. It was all over now. This Mr. Hendricks would undoubtedly call the Population Police, and she'd be arrested all over again. This time, she was sure, the hating man wouldn't give her any more chances to prove herself. The only thing Nina could hope for now was that somehow Percy, Matthias, and Alia could avoid being caught, too. Somehow she'd have to warn them. . . .

"So, you're not talking?" Mr. Hendricks said. "Perhaps my young friends here might tell me what they observed, and we'll go from there."

"Sir," Lee began. "We caught her eating our corn. And

she was putting lots of our vegetables into her bag there."

Nina realized she still had the old, smelly burlap bag slung around her neck. Quickly, before anyone might ask how one girl could possibly eat all that food, she said, "I was hungry. Very hungry."

"Ah," Mr. Hendricks said. "Now we hear an excuse." He squinted, seeming to look far off into the distance. He shook his head, ever so slightly, his thick white hair barely moving. "Boys, I believe I can handle this situation by myself now. Why don't you take her into the living room and then go resume your posts?"

Nina wondered what "resume your posts" meant. Both boys nodded. Lee tugged on Nina's arm and muttered, "Come on."

Once they were in the living room—the fanciest place Nina had ever seen, crowded with heavy wood furniture—Lee half shoved Nina toward a couch. Nina realized she'd probably never see Lee again.

"Lee," she whispered. "You probably won't believe me, but . . . I didn't try to betray you. I didn't know what Jason was doing. Would you . . . would you tell the others? So they can remember me the right way?"

Lee didn't say yes or no, only backed away. Nina couldn't even be sure that he'd heard her. She didn't expect anyone to think too highly of her—she wasn't Jen Talbot, hero for the cause of third children everywhere. But she hoped that Sally and Bonner, at least, wouldn't live the rest of their lives thinking of her as a traitor. She hoped that if the

Hendricks School boys and the Harlow School girls ever started meeting in the woods again, they wouldn't pass down stories of Jason and Nina, equally deceptive, equally evil.

After Lee and Trey left, Mr. Hendricks rolled into the living room. He pulled the wooden door mostly shut behind him.

"Now," he said. "Perhaps you'll be a bit more forthcoming without an audience."

Nina's gaze darted around the room, taking in the unlatched door, the thick glass in the windows, the picture frames and heavy knickknacks on the tables. She was looking for an escape. Maybe a weapon, too. What would happen if she threw a ceramic bird at a man in a wheelchair? Could she hit him? Would it do any good?

Nina looked Mr. Hendricks over carefully. Despite the white hair, he was hardly old and decrepit. She even suspected the wheelchair was just a fake, meant to deceive her into thinking she could overpower him easily. Probably he was as strong and muscular as Lee and Trey. Probably . . .

Nina's glance reached Mr. Hendricks's feet—or rather, the empty space where his feet should have been. He didn't have any feet.

He can't chase me, Nina thought. *If I can escape . . .*

But he would call for help. He'd have a search party ready in a matter of minutes.

But minutes are all I need to warn Percy, Matthias, and Alia. . . .

"Well?" Mr. Hendricks said.

Nina sprang up from the couch, grabbed the back of the wheelchair, and dumped it forward, spilling Mr. Hendricks to the floor. She dashed out the living room door, out the front door, down the front steps. She worried about running into Lee and Trey—where were their "posts," by the garden?—but her feet flew so quickly, everything was a blur. She couldn't watch for them or anyone else.

Before she knew it, she was crashing into the woods, toward the glade where she'd left the others waiting for food.

"Percy! Matthias! Alia!" she called. "I have to warn you. . . ." The words wouldn't come quickly enough between her gasps for air.

Alia popped out from behind a tree.

"Nina!" she scolded. "You're making too much noise. Someone will hear you!"

"It . . . doesn't . . . matter," she panted. She stopped running, caught her breath. She saw that Matthias and Percy were staring out at her from the shadows behind a bush. "They caught me. I escaped again, but they'll probably be looking for me soon. I had to warn you. . . ." She took another deep breath. Her brain still felt starved for oxygen. "This isn't a safe place anymore. You'll have to go somewhere else. But you can. You guys are smart."

"Nina," Alia protested. "Come with us, then—"

"No," Nina said. "I'd be . . . dangerous to you. They know to look for me now. I probably don't have much time. But

I wanted to tell you . . . the hating man. In prison. He put me in your cell to betray you. He wanted me to tell him all your secrets. And I might have. If we hadn't escaped, I—"

"But you didn't," Matthias said. "You didn't tell the Population Police anything."

"I wanted to," Nina said. "Jason betrayed me, and I wanted to hurt someone else. And I wanted to save my life. . . ."

"It's all right," Alia said, stepping closer.

"And I don't blame you for never trusting me," Nina continued. "I wasn't trustworthy. Even that first night in the woods, when I was supposed to be sitting sentry, I fell asleep." It was such a relief to confess that, even that. "I never really trusted you, either. The last time I had friends, they didn't help me at all when I was arrested. So I thought . . ."

Nina was crying. Between being caught and running away—and, probably, because of having nothing to eat in days but vegetables—she felt dizzy and light-headed. But it was important for her to tell the others everything. All her stories spilled out. Probably the others could make no sense of what she said. Tales of playing dolls with Aunty Zenka were all mixed up with tales of meeting the Hendricks School boys in the woods with Sally and Bonner.

"I want you to know my real name, too," Nina said. "It's Elodie. When you remember me, remember Elodie."

The woods were dark when Nina finished talking. She

was just lucky she hadn't been found immediately. She couldn't see the others' faces, couldn't tell what they thought of her stream of words. But for practically the first time since she'd been arrested, Nina was sure she'd done the exact right thing. The others were going to be safe now. And she'd told them the truth.

"You should go now," she said. "Oh—here." She pulled the grungy food bag from around her neck and handed it to Alia. "There's not much in it because . . . well, something's better than nothing, isn't it?"

The tears flowed down her face. She reached down and drew Alia into a hug. Percy and Matthias stepped forward, too, and threw their arms around both girls. All four kids stood together, swaying slightly, holding one another up.

Nina had her eyes shut, squeezing out the tears. But through her tears she suddenly saw a glimmer of light off to the right. She pulled away from the hug, stared off toward a flashlight bobbing in the woods. Then she saw other flashlights, circling closer and closer.

"They're looking for me!" she hissed. "Go on! Hide somewhere far away from me."

Nina didn't have time to make sure that the others had moved out of sight. For, seconds later, a flashlight shone right in her face and a booming voice cried out, "Nina Idi! Fancy meeting you here!"

It was the hating man.

CHAPTER TWENTY-SEVEN

Terrified, Nina turned to run. But something clawed at her arm, something held on to her leg. She tumbled forward, sprawled across the ground.

"Let go of me!" she roared, though it must have been a vine tangled around her ankle, must have been a branch scratching against her arm. Nina tried to scramble up, but it was too late. The flashlight shone in her eyes; when the hating man's voice came again, it was practically in her ear.

"Nina, Nina, Nina," he said. "It's all over now."

Nina struggled to sit up. It was Percy who was holding onto her arm, Matthias who was holding onto her leg.

They had betrayed her, too. They were turning her in to the hating man.

Alia stepped up beside the boys, smiling at Nina. Nina's eyes swam with tears. Not Alia, too. Nina couldn't take the thought that Alia had betrayed her as well.

"No," Nina moaned. Then she screamed, "No!"

Nina didn't care who heard. Behind the hating man she could see the shapes of perhaps a dozen people, all with flashlights shining right at her. Their faces were completely in shadow, impossible to make out.

Alia leaned into the circle of light with Nina.

"You're safe now," she said happily. "You passed the test."

Nina shook her head violently, not wanting to believe the evidence in front of her eyes.

"Alia, run," Nina whispered. She wasn't sure which she wanted more—for the little girl to be safe, or for Alia merely to prove that she was scared, too, and hadn't helped betraying Nina. Alia didn't move. Nina hoped she just hadn't heard. "Alia, you have to escape. That man is from the Population Police. He's the hating man!"

"No, he's not," a familiar voice called out from the shadows. "He only pretends to work for the Population Police. He's Mr. Talbot. Jen Talbot's dad." Lee Grant stepped forward and bent down beside Nina. "Remember who Jen Talbot is?"

"Of course I do," Nina snapped. "She's the hero for the cause of third children everywhere. Jason used to tell us about her all the time. But . . ."

She wondered suddenly if that was a lie, too, if there'd never been a Jen Talbot, or if she hadn't been a hero. Dazedly Nina looked around at the faces circling her. Everyone came forward, crowding close. Percy and Matthias lifted Nina up to see, instead of holding her back. Lee and Trey and a few other Hendricks School boys stood in a clump off to the right.

The hating man—Mr. Talbot?—cleared his throat.

"It's true, what Lee said," he began. "I am a double agent working for the Population Police, but only in order to double-cross them. Back in the spring I faced a dilemma. A boy at Hendricks School for Boys told the Population Police he knew of several shadow children at the school who were using fake identities and pretending to be legitimate. If this boy managed to convince the Population Police that he was telling the truth, I knew several children would die. Thanks to young Lee Grant over there, as well as some quick-thinking administrators, we managed to foil his plan.

"But this boy—Jason, as you all know—said he had an accomplice at the girls' school. Nina Idi. You. We arrested you as well. But the longer I spent interrogating you, the more convinced I became that you were truly innocent and actually knew nothing of Jason's plan. But I couldn't be entirely sure, and it was a matter of life and death that I be absolutely, one hundred percent certain."

"Yeah. My life. My death," Nina grumbled, still too dazed to think straight.

"And many others'," Mr. Talbot said. "You knew the truth about dozens of kids."

Every girl at Harlow School, Nina thought. *And lots of boys at Hendricks. I knew they were all former shadow children. Did everyone really think that I might betray them?*

"About the same time, a Population Police informer in the capital had turned in three kids who were involved in manufacturing fake I.D.'s,—Percy, Matthias, and Alia. I figured they were safer in prison than out on the streets, for the time being. Their protector, Samuel Jones, had been killed in the rally for third-children rights in April."

"That's who 'Sa—' was. You almost said his name once," Nina said, almost to herself.

"He took in third children," Alia whispered. "When our parents abandoned us. He raised us. He took care of us."

"I thought you said God took care of you," Nina scoffed. She sounded just like Aunty Lystra at her most skeptical.

"Who do you think Samuel was working for?" Alia said.

Nina kept shaking her head, as if she could deny everything she heard.

"Percy and Matthias had promised Samuel to stay away from the rally to protect Alia," Mr. Talbot said. "So they alone were spared, and they alone were still around to be betrayed. Then later, in prison, they agreed to help me give you a test, to see which side you were really on. If you had betrayed them, we would have known you couldn't be trusted. If you protected them . . . we'd save you."

Nina gasped, finally beginning to make sense of his words. If the hating man didn't really believe in the Population Police's cause—if he was a double agent working against them—then everything was backward.

"So, if I'd double-crossed them, trying to save my own life . . . you would have killed me?" Nina asked.

"Yes," Mr. Talbot said.

Nina thought about how close she'd come to betraying

the others, how miserable she'd been in prison, how willing she'd been to do almost anything to save herself.

"I didn't do it," she said. "I could have, but I didn't."

"But you didn't refuse to betray them, either," Mr. Talbot said. "You weren't committing yourself either way. We had to add a more dangerous part to the test."

Nina couldn't figure out what he meant. Then she remembered the guard, Mack, sprawling across the table, his ring of keys sliding right toward Nina.

"You let us escape," Nina accused, as if it were a crime. "You let me get the keys and have a way out, and made me think I was figuring out everything on my own. Why, I bet . . . I bet Mack wasn't even sick."

Mr. Talbot chuckled. "No, but he put on a good act, didn't he?"

"And then"—Nina was still putting everything together—"the other three kids knew that I might offer to help them escape. Why wasn't that enough? Why didn't you trust me then?"

She thought about the past—was it weeks?—of sleeping outside, of living on stale, moldy food or dirty raw vegetables. Could she have avoided all that?

"We still weren't sure about you," Percy said in his usual logical tone. "It was possible that you were only taking us along because you were scared to go on your own. You might have just been using us."

Nina remembered how unconcerned the others had been when they ran out of food, how little they had cared about making plans for the future. No wonder. They were waiting on her. Waiting on her to prove herself.

"When we met the policemen by the river—," she said.

"That was part of the test," Mr. Talbot said. "Those weren't policemen. They were people working with our cause."

"And I passed that test?" Nina asked.

"Sort of," Mr. Talbot said. "You didn't try to turn the others in. But we still weren't sure of your motives."

Nina shivered, thinking about how closely she'd been watched all along. Every time she complained about their rocky, uneven "beds" in the woods. Every time she griped about the dirty vegetables.

"I bet the rest of you were getting food somewhere else," she said.

"Not much," Alia said in a small voice, looking down. She looked back up at Nina, her eyes flashing. "*I* thought you were good. I wanted to tell. But these guys"—she pointed at Percy, Matthias, and Mr. Talbot—"they said I had to wait until you told us everything. Until you told us that you were supposed to betray us to the Population Police."

"I did that tonight," Nina said wonderingly. She looked around again at the circle of people, the circle of light in the dark woods.

She remembered how panicked she'd been, running out to the woods only minutes earlier. She hadn't been thinking at all of saving her own life. She'd only wanted to save Percy, Matthias, and Alia.

But she hadn't cared that much about them back when she first met them, when she offered them a chance to escape, when she saw the fake policemen by the river.

"You gave me a lot of chances," she said to Mr. Talbot.

"I thought you deserved them," he said. "You didn't deserve what happened to you before."

Nina remembered the day she was arrested, how nobody had spoken out on her behalf as she glided forward in the dining hall. She remembered how much she'd trusted Jason, and then he had betrayed her. No, she hadn't deserved that. Nobody did. What she deserved was the way Gran and the aunties had loved her, the way they'd hidden her even though they might have been killed for it. But Alia, Percy, and Matthias hadn't deserved being betrayed, either. They hadn't deserved weeks in a dark prison cell, weeks sleeping outdoors on rocks and twigs and itchy leaves. But they'd endured all of that, willingly, for her. They'd agreed to endure all of that before they even knew if she was good or bad.

Nina's eyes filled up with tears, but they weren't tears of fear or panic or sorrow now. They were tears of joy.

"Thank you," she whispered, and the words seemed to encompass everyone in front of her—Percy, Matthias, and Alia, Mr. Talbot, even Lee and Trey. But the words were more powerful than that. Her whisper seemed to fly through the night, through the dark. Somewhere, far away, she could even imagine Gran and the aunties hearing her, too.

CHAPTER TWENTY-EIGHT

Nina stood beside Lee Grant, pulling corn from a row of stalks.

"Leave the small ears to grow," Lee cautioned. "We only need enough for the feast tonight."

"Only?" Nina laughed. "There'll be twenty people there!"

"Forty ears, then," Lee countered. "That's not much. Back home, when my mom was canning corn, we used to pick—"

"What? Forty million?" Nina teased.

In the days since she'd been caught, she'd been staying at Mr. Hendricks's house with Percy, Matthias, and Alia. But she'd spent a lot of time with Lee and already listened to dozens of "back home" stories. She didn't know what it was like at Harlow School for Girls, but at Hendricks, boys were not pretending so much to be their fake identities. They were telling the truth more.

Nina jerked another ear from a stalk.

"Anyway, forget forty ears," she said. "If you're figuring two per person, that's only thirty-eight. I don't think I'll ever be able to eat corn again, not after the way you scared me in the garden last week, midbite."

"More for me," Lee said, clowning a selfish grab around all the corn they'd picked so far.

Nina wondered if this was how normal children acted—children who'd never had to hide. She guessed she'd have a chance to find out now. She, Percy, Matthias, and Alia were being sent on to another school, one where third children with fake I.D.'s mixed with firstborns and secondborns. That was why they were having a feast tonight, a combination of a celebration and a farewell.

"Given how things happened, Harlow School is probably not the best place for you anymore," Mr. Hendricks had told Nina.

Nina had had another flash of remembering that horrific canyon of eyes, watching her walk to her doom.

"I . . . I think I can forgive the other girls," she had said. "Now."

"But are they ready to forgive you?" Mr. Hendricks asked. "No matter how much you reassure them, how much the officials reassure them, there will always be someone who suspects that you just got off, that you really were working with Jason. They haven't . . . grown up like you have."

And Nina understood. She wasn't the same lovesick, easily terrified child she'd been at Harlow School. That was why she liked talking to Lee now. He'd grown up a lot, too. The other boys looked up to him. They didn't even call him Lee anymore. He was mostly L.G.—and they said it reverently.

Nina still called him Lee. She didn't like too many things changing.

"Nina," Lee said now, slowly peeling back the husk of an ear of corn to check for rot. "Before you leave tomorrow, there's something I've been wanting to tell you."

"What?"

Lee tossed the ear of corn onto the pile with the rest. It must have been okay.

"I've been thinking about Jason," he said.

Nina stiffened just hearing that name. She might be able to forgive her friends at Harlow, but she wasn't ready to forgive Jason.

"So?" she asked.

"Well, I was thinking about what I heard him say on the phone to the Population Police that night he was turning everyone in. He made it sound like you were working with him."

"I know," Nina said. "That's how I ended up in prison." She couldn't keep the bitterness out of her voice.

In one clean jerk Lee pulled another ear from another stalk.

"But I don't think Jason was saying that to get you in trouble. He didn't expect to be arrested, to have you arrested. He meant for the illegal third children with fake I.D.'s to be arrested. I think . . . I think he was actually trying to save you."

Nina reeled backward, stunned beyond words. Lee took one look at Nina's face and kept explaining.

"Don't you see?" he said. "It wouldn't have made any sense for Jason to say you were working with him if he wanted to get you in trouble. He thought he—and you—were going to be rewarded. He was . . . he was maybe trying to protect you from ever being turned in by anyone else. See, if years from now someone accused you of being illegal, he could pop up and say, 'Nina? How could Nina be an exnay? She helped turn them in!' "

Lee did such a good job of imitating Jason's voice that Nina could almost believe. But only almost.

"Jason was doing something wrong. Evil. He wanted innocent kids to die," she said harshly. She pulled so hard on an ear of corn that the whole stalk came out of the ground.

Lee frowned but didn't say anything about his precious cornstalk.

"Yeah. Believe me, I was pretty mad at Jason myself. But I'm just saying—I don't think he was all bad. I think he, um, really liked you. And that was why he was trying to save you."

Nina stood still, trying to make sense of Lee's words. It flip-flopped everything she'd thought for the past few months. How could she accept Lee's explanation? How could Jason have been so evil yet tried to save her?

For a minute she almost believed. Then she remembered.

"Mr. Talbot had a tape," she said dully. "Of Jason confessing. And he was lying and saying it was all my fault, that I was the one who wanted to turn in the exnays."

"Oh, Mr. Talbot could have faked that tape," Lee said. "I've seen him fake pictures."

"But it was Jason's voice," Nina said. "I heard him. I heard the tape!"

Lee turned back to the garden.

"Go ask him," he said with a shrug.

Nina stood still for a moment, then she dropped her corn and took off running. Hope swelled in her heart. She burst into Mr. Hendricks's cottage and dashed into the living room, where Mr. Hendricks and Mr. Talbot were conferring.

"The tape," she said. "Of Jason betraying me. Lying. Was it real?"

Mr. Talbot turned around slowly, looked at her blankly.

"You had a tape," she repeated breathlessly. "In prison. Of Jason saying it was my idea to betray exnays, my idea to turn them in to the Population Police. Did he really say that? Or did you fake the tape?"

Mr. Talbot blinked.

"Does it matter?" he asked.

"Of course it matters!" Nina shrieked.

Mr. Talbot raised one eyebrow.

"Why?" he said.

Nina had so many reasons, they jumbled together.

"If he didn't betray me, if he was really trying to help

me—then he really loved me. Then Aunty Zenka was right, and love is everything, and the world's a good place. And I can be happy remembering him. But if he betrayed me—how can I think about the time we had together without hating him? How can I ever trust anyone, ever again?"

"You've believed for months that he betrayed you," Mr. Talbot said. "And you still trusted Percy, Matthias, and Alia. You've been acting like you trust Lee and Trey and Mr. Hendricks and me. Don't you?"

"Yes, but . . ." Nina couldn't explain. "Maybe I shouldn't trust you. You've lied to me a lot."

Nina was surprised when both Mr. Talbot and Mr. Hendricks burst out laughing.

"It's not funny," she protested.

Mr. Talbot stopped laughing, and sighed. "Nina, we live in complicated times. I would have loved it if that first time I talked to you in your prison cell, I could have come straight out and said, 'Here's the deal. I hate the Population Police. What about you?' And it would have been great if I could have been sure that you would give me an honest answer. But—can you really see that happening? Don't you see how muddy everyone's intentions get, how people end up doing the wrong things for the right reasons, and the right things for the wrong reasons—and all any of us can do is try our hardest and have faith that somehow, someday, it will all work out?"

Nina looked down at her hands, still splotched with mud from the garden. She looked back up.

"Was the tape fake or not?" she asked again.

Mr. Talbot looked straight back at her.

"It was fake," he said quietly. "Some of our tech people spliced it together."

A grin burst out over Nina's face. "So Lee was right. Jason did love me," she whispered in wonderment.

Mr. Talbot and Mr. Hendricks exchanged glances in such a way that Nina felt like she was back with Percy, Matthias, and Alia.

"So that's enough for you?" Mr. Talbot asked. "It doesn't matter that Jason was trying to get other kids killed? You don't care about the evil he did as long as he loved *you*?"

Nina's smile slipped. Why did Mr. Talbot have to confuse everything again?

"No, no," she said. "That's not what I believe. This just means—he wasn't all bad. He's dead anyway. So I can . . . hold on to the good memories and let go of being mad at him." She wondered what had made Jason the way he was. She remembered how desperate she'd felt in the jail cell when she'd been so tempted to betray Percy, Matthias, and Alia. What if Jason had been even more desperate? What if he hadn't wanted to betray anyone, either, but had been too weak to resist?

It was odd to think of Jason as weak. She could actually feel sorry for him now. She could hold on to that forever, the way she held on to memories of Gran and the aunties.

"Nina," Mr. Talbot said. "Jason isn't dead. I thought they had executed him, but . . . it turns out that another faction of the Population Police thought he might still be useful. I've only recently found out that he's working for the Population Police in some top secret project. Something we who oppose the Government are very concerned about." He paused for a second, as if waiting for the news to sink in. "So, what does that information do for you? Are you going to rush to his side, to help him, because he *loves* you?"

Nina stared at Mr. Talbot in amazement.

"He's alive?" she whimpered. "He's alive?"

Strangely, this seemed like bad news. If Jason were dead, she could go all misty-eyed remembering him, daydreaming about what might have been, just like Aunty Zenka mooning over one of her books. But with him alive and working for the Population Police—"I have to stay mad," she said aloud. "I can't ever forgive him."

"Bitter is a bad way to live," Mr. Talbot said.

Nina remembered that he had lost Jen, that he had reason to stay angry at the Government forever. She sank down onto one of Mr. Hendricks's couches. This was all going to overwhelm her. She was just a little girl who'd spent most of her life hiding, listening to old ladies' foolish stories. Or had they been foolish? All the fairy tales Gran and the aunties had told her were about people staying true to what was right in the face of great adversity. She'd heard the wrong part of the stories if she thought she was just supposed to sit around like a princess, waiting for some prince to fall in love with her.

She looked straight at Mr. Talbot.

"I don't want to stay bitter. But I want to help you—what can I do to make sure Jason's project fails?"

Mr. Talbot almost smiled. Nina felt like she'd passed another test.

"We'll see," he said. "We'll see."

Nina went back out toward Lee's garden to finish picking corn. The sun was setting now, casting long shadows over the path. Just about every step Nina took alternated between sunlight and dark. Nina's thoughts bounced back and forth just as dramatically. *Jason* did *love me. That's what really matters.... But he was still evil.... Why did I say I'd help Mr. Talbot oppose the Government?... How could I not have said that, after everything Mr. Talbot did for me?... What can I possibly do, anyway?*

As Nina approached the garden she saw Lee waiting for her there. Whatever she did for Mr. Talbot, she realized, she would not be alone. Lee would probably be involved, and so would Percy and Matthias and Alia.

Nina remembered how alone she'd felt in her jail cell, all those months ago. Feeling abandoned and betrayed was worse than hunger, worse than cold, worse than the handcuffs on her wrists. But she hadn't been abandoned; she had only accidentally been betrayed.

"Well?" Lee said as soon as she got close enough to hear. "Was I right?"

It took Nina a moment to remember what he was talking about: the tape. Jason's betrayal.

"It's a long story," Nina said. "And it's not over yet."

But part of her story was over—the part where she was innocent and stupid and useless. She'd been so worried before that people might not remember her as Elodie—sweet, loving, little-girl Elodie. But she'd outgrown Elodie. She'd outgrown Nina the ninny, too. She was ready now to make whatever name she carried one that people could respect and revere.

Like Jen Talbot's.

"I think . . . I think I just volunteered to help Mr. Talbot and Mr. Hendricks fight the Population Police," she said.

Lee's gaze was steady and unfailing.

"Good," he said. "Welcome to the club."

Here's a look at Margaret Peterson Haddix's book *Found*, which launches her new series, The Missing.

Available now from
Simon & Schuster Books for Young Readers

PROLOGUE

It wasn't there. Then it was.

Later, that was how Angela DuPre would describe the airplane—over and over, to one investigator after another—until she was told never to speak of it again.

But when she first saw the plane that night, she wasn't thinking about mysteries or secrets. She was wondering how many mistakes she could make without getting fired, how many questions she dared ask before her supervisor, Monique, would explode, "That's it! You're too stupid to work at Sky Trails Air! Get out of here!" Angela had used a Post-it note to write down the code for standby passengers who'd received a seat assignment at the last minute, and she'd stuck it to her computer screen. She knew she had. But somehow, between the flight arriving from Saint Louis and the one leaving for Chicago, the Post-it had vanished. Any minute now, she thought, some standby passenger would show up at the counter asking for a boarding pass, and Angela would be forced to turn to Monique once more and mumble, "Uh, what was that code again?" And then Monique, who had perfect hair and perfect nails and a perfect tan and had probably been born knowing all the Sky Trails codes, would grit her teeth and narrow her eyes and repeat the code in that slow fake-patient voice she'd been using with Angela all night, the voice that said behind the words, *I know you're severely mentally challenged, so I will try not to speak faster than one word per minute, but you have to realize, this is a real strain for me because I am so vastly superior. . . .*

Angela was not severely mentally challenged. She'd done fine in school and at the Sky Trails orientation. It was just, this was her first actual day on the job, and Monique had been nasty from the very start. Every one of Monique's frowns and glares and insinuations kept making Angela feel more panicky and stupid.

Sighing, Angela glanced up. She needed a break from staring at the computer screen longing for a lost Post-it. She peered out at the passengers crowding the terminal: tired-looking families sprawled in seats, dark-suited businessmen sprinting down the aisle. Which one of them would be the standby flier who'd rush up to the counter and ruin Angela's life? Generally speaking, Angela had always liked people; she wasn't used to seeing them as threats. She forced her gaze beyond the clumps of passengers, to the huge plate glass window on the other side of the aisle. It was getting dark out, and Angela could see the runway lights twinkling in the distance.

Runway, runaway, she thought vaguely. And then—had she blinked?—suddenly the lights were gone. No, she corrected herself, *blocked.* Suddenly there was an airplane between Angela and the runway lights, an airplane rolling rapidly toward the terminal.

Angela gasped.

"What now?" Monique snarled, her voice thick with exasperation.

"That plane," Angela said. "At gate 2B. I thought it—" What was she supposed to say? *Wasn't there? Appeared out of thin air?*"—I thought it was going too fast and might run into the building," she finished in a rush, because suddenly that had seemed true too. She watched as the plane pulled to a stop, neatly aligned with the jetway. "But it . . . didn't. No worries."

Monique whirled on Angela.

"Never," she began, in a hushed voice full of suppressed rage, "never, ever, ever say anything like that. Weren't you paying attention in orientation? Never say you think a plane is going to crash. Never say a plane could crash. Never even use the word *crash*. Do you understand?"

"Okay," Angela whispered. "Sorry."

But some small rebellious part of her brain was thinking, *I didn't use the word* crash. *Weren't you paying attention to me? And if a plane really was going to run into the building, wouldn't Sky Trails want its employees to warn people, to get them out of the way?*

Just as rebelliously, Angela kept watching the plane parked at 2B, instead of bending her head back down to concentrate on her computer.

"Um, Monique?" she said after a few moments. "Should one of us go over there and help the passengers unload—er, I mean—deplane?" She was proud of herself for remembering to use the official airline-sanctioned word for unloading.

Beside her, Monique rolled her eyes.

"The gate agents responsible for 2B," she said in a tight voice, "will handle deplaning there."

Angela glanced at the 2B counter, which was silent and dark and completely unattended. There wasn't even a message scrolling across the LCD sign behind the counter to indicate that the plane had arrived or where it'd come from.

"Nobody's there," Angela said stubbornly.

Frowning, Monique finally glanced up.

"Great. Just great," she muttered. "I always have to fix everyone else's mistakes." She began stabbing her perfectly manicured nails at her computer keyboard. Then she stopped, mid-stab. "Wait—that can't be right."

"What is it?" Angela asked.

Monique was shaking her head.

"Must be pilot error," she said, grimacing in disgust. "Some yahoo pulled up to the wrong gate. There's not supposed to be anyone at that gate until the Cleveland flight at nine thirty."

Angela considered telling Monique that if Sky Trails had banned *crash* from their employees' vocabulary, that maybe passengers should be protected from hearing *pilot error* as well. But Monique was already grabbing the telephone, barking out orders.

"Yeah, Bob, major screwup," she was saying. "You've got to get someone over here. . . . No, I don't know which gate it was supposed to go to. How would I know? Do you think I'm clairvoyant? . . . No, I can't see the numbers on the plane. Don't you know it's dark out?"

With her free hand, Monique was gesturing frantically at Angela.

"At least go open the door!" she hissed.

"You mean . . ."

"The door to the jetway!" Monique said, pointing. Angela hoped that some of the contempt on Monique's face was intended for Bob, not just her. Angela imagined meeting Bob someday, sharing a laugh at Monique's expense. Still, dutifully, she walked over to the 2B waiting area and pulled open the door to the hallway that led down to the plane.

Nobody came out.

Angela picked a piece of lint off her blue skirt and then stood at attention, her back perfectly straight, just like in the training videos. Maybe she couldn't keep track of standby codes, but she was capable of standing up straight.

Still, nobody appeared.

Angela began to feel foolish, standing so alertly by an open door that no one was using. She bent her head and peeked down the jetway—it was deserted and turned at such an angle that she couldn't see all the way down to the plane, to see if anyone had opened the door to the jet yet. She backed up a little and peered out the window, straight down to the cockpit of the plane. The cockpit was dark, its windows blank, and that struck Angela as odd. She'd been on the job for only five hours, and she'd been a little distracted. But she was pretty sure that when planes landed, the pilots stayed in the cockpit for a while filling out paperwork or something. She thought that they at least waited until all the passengers were off before they turned out the cockpit lights.

Angela peeked down the empty jetway once more and went back to Monique.

"Of course I'm sure there's a plane at that gate! I can see it with my own eyes!" Monique was practically screaming into the phone. She shook her head at Angela, and for the first time it was almost in a companionable way, as if to say, *At least you know there's a plane there! Unlike the other morons I have to deal with!* Monique cupped her hand over the receiver and fumed to Angela, "The incompetence around here is unbelievable! The control tower says that plane never landed, never showed up on the radar. The Sky Trails dispatcher says we're not missing a plane—everything that was supposed to land in the past hour pulled up to the right gate, and all the other planes due to arrive within the next hour or so are accounted for. How could so many people just lose a plane?"

Or, how could we find it? Angela thought. The whole situation was beginning to seem strange to her, otherworldly. But maybe that was just a function of being new to the job, of having spent so much time concentrating on the computer and being yelled at by Monique. Maybe airports lost and found planes all the time, and that was just one of those things nobody had mentioned in the Sky Trails orientation.

"Did, uh, anybody try to contact the pilot?" Angela asked cautiously.

"Of course!" Monique said. "But there's no answer. He must be on the wrong frequency."

Angela thought of the dark cockpit, the way she hadn't been able to see through the windows. She decided not to mention this.

"Should I go back and wait? . . ."

Monique nodded fiercely and went back to yelling into the phone: "What do you mean, this isn't your responsibility? It's not my responsibility either!"

Angela was glad to put a wide aisle and two waiting areas between herself and Monique again. She went back to the jetway door by gate 2B. The sloped hallway leading down to the plane was still empty, and the colorful travel posters lining the walls—"Sky Trails! Your ticket to the world!"—seemed jarringly bright. Angela stepped into the jetway.

I'll just go down far enough to see if the jet door is open, she told herself. *It may be a violation of protocol, but Monique won't notice, not when she's busy yelling at everyone else in the airport. . . .*

At the bend in the ramp, Angela looked around the corner. She had a limited view, but caught a quick glimpse of a flight attendants' little galley, with neatly stowed drink carts. Obviously, the jet door was standing wide open. She started to turn around, already beginning to debate with herself about whether she should report this information to Monique. Then she heard—what? A whimper? A cry?

Angela couldn't exactly identify the sound, but it was enough to pull her on down the jetway.

New Sky Trails employee saves passenger on first day on job, she thought to herself, imagining the praise and congratulations—and maybe the raise—she'd be sure to receive if what she was visualizing was real. She'd learned CPR in the orientation session. She knew basic first aid. She knew where every emergency phone in the airport was located. She started walking faster, then running.

On the side of the jet, she was surprised to see a strange insignia: TACHYON TRAVEL, it said, some airline Angela had never heard of. Was that a private charter company maybe? And then, while she was staring at it, the words suddenly changed into the familiar wing-in-the-clouds symbol of Sky Trails.

Angela blinked.

That couldn't have happened, she told herself. *It was just an optical illusion, just because I was running, just because I'm worried about whoever made that cry or whimper. . . .*

Angela stepped onto the plane. She turned her head

first to the left, looking into the cockpit. Its door also stood open, but the small space was empty, the instruments dark.

"Hello?" Angela called, looking to the right now, expecting to see some flight attendant with perfectly applied makeup—or maybe some flight attendant and a pilot bent over a prone passenger, maybe an old man suddenly struck down by a heart attack or a stroke. Or, at the very least, passengers crowding the aisle, clutching laptops and stuffed animals brought from faraway grandparents' homes, overtired toddlers crying, fragile old women calling out to taller men, "Could you pull my luggage down from the overhead for me? It's that red suitcase over there. . . ."

But the aisle of this airplane was as empty and silent as its cockpit. Angela could see all the way to the back of the plane, and not a single person stood in her view, not a single voice answered her.

Only then did Angela drop her gaze to the passenger seats. They stretched back twelve rows, with two seats per row on the left side of the aisle and one each on the right. She stepped forward, peering at all of them. Thirty-six seats on this plane, and every single one of them was full.

Each seat contained a baby.